Lily

Lily and Georgie raced along the passage to the orangery, flinging the glass doors open, and stumbled out through the night gardens. It was a moonlit night, but still the overgrown garden seemed full of confused and disturbing shapes, which only resolved themselves into familiar landmarks as they dashed past.

Lily risked a glance back at the house, its dark bulk shining here and there with tiny lights. One of the lights was moving now across the dining room windows.

'She's gone to Mama. They'll be after us any minute,' Lily hissed to Georgie. 'Run faster!'

Lily

HOLLY WEBB

ORCHARD

ORCHARD BOOKS
338 Euston Road, London NW1 3BH
Orchard Books Australia
Level 17/207 Kent Street, Sydney, NSW 2000

First published in the UK in 2011 by Orchard Books

ISBN 978 1 40831 349 7

Text © Holly Webb 2011

A CIP catalogue record for this book is available from the British Library.

1 3 5 7 9 10 8 6 4 2

Printed in Great Britain

Orchard Books is a division of Hachette Children's Books,
an Hachette UK company.

www.hachette.co.uk

For Alice, Sydney and Tom

ONE

Lily stared out across the water. It was very early – she wasn't sure of the time exactly, but the maids had only just been lighting the stove when she scurried out of the back door of Merrythought House. It was full summer, and the sun was hot already, glittering on the ripples. The hard, silvery light seemed to cut a path across the grey-blue sea, so clear a path that it looked almost solid, and Lily longed to step out onto it, and walk across. She stretched out a foot, even, without realising it, and might have stepped into the water, if Peter hadn't snorted in disgust at her silliness, and grabbed her elbow.

Lily blinked and turned to look him. His arms were folded now, and he was eyeing her, his nose wrinkled up as though he were trying not to laugh. She glared back at him. 'What? I wasn't actually going to!'

She sighed, and sat down on the warm stones, opening her book again. She didn't really understand it – it was a great fat thing about the practice of glamours that she'd found in the china cupboard – but she was trying to. She *ought* to be able to understand. Both her parents were magicians, after all. And her sister was a genius at this sort of thing. So why couldn't Lily even grow her fingernails a little longer? She stretched out her fingers, but the nails stayed stubby and short, and rather dirty. Lily sighed again, crossly, and gazed out over the water, the view pulling her from the book once more.

From this angle, the path was only sunshine on the sea, and the mainland was the merest smudge of a shadow on the horizon.

'It did look real, though, didn't it?' she said quietly to Peter. 'I wonder what it's like, over there.'

Peter stomped away across the stones, and Lily flinched at the angry clatter of the pebbles under his feet. She sometimes forgot that he hadn't been born on the island, as she had. He knew what the mainland was like, and she shouldn't have made him remember.

She sprang up, and followed him back to the cliff path, toiling up towards the house. He would have been missed by now, probably. He was stronger than she was, and he reached the top of the path before her, turning to wave once before he raced off over the lawn. Lily didn't hurry to catch up with him. It was better that they didn't go back together – Peter wasn't supposed to be spending his time *running after that dratted girl*. Lily had heard Mrs Porter, the cook, say so the day before. She wandered through the long grass, kicking at dandelion clocks, and watching the seeds puff away on the wind. How far could they fly? They were too hard to follow against the white light of the sky, but perhaps some would float for miles, and grow Merrythought dandelions across the sea.

She was approaching the house, her hands full of dandelions now, blowing the seeds up into the sky, when she stopped dead, her breath catching in her throat. The warmth of the sun seemed to seep away.

A figure had appeared round the corner of the house, too quickly somehow, as though she hadn't walked, just was suddenly *there*.

Lily forced herself to smile a little, and nod, even though she was trembling, and the woman in the dark dress bowed politely, and stood back for her to pass. It was only proper, as she was a lady's maid, and Lily was a daughter of the house, but it felt wrong. Lily scurried away, hurrying round the corner. She could feel Marten staring after her, and her gaze clung.

Lily had never been sure what it was about Marten that frightened her so much. Perhaps the black clothes – Marten never wore anything else. A black wool dress, winter and summer, and a veil and gloves, even in the house. The other servants muttered about odd foreign habits, but they were used to her. Marten had been Lily's mother's maid for years.

Once she had turned the corner, onto the path that led to the back of the house, and the kitchens, Lily flattened herself into the shadows along the wall, gasping. She wasn't usually so cowardly, but Marten had crept up on her – or it felt like it. She gulped air, feeling dizzy, and then bolted for the kitchens, wanting warmth, and light, and company, however bad-tempered it might be.

Even though Mrs Porter was in the middle of one of her tirades, the kitchen still felt welcoming after the sudden shadow outside. Peter had been missed then, Lily noted guiltily, as she realised who Mrs Porter was shouting at.

'Lazy, good-for-nothing boy! Off gallivanting, when we're near out of firewood! I need to cook madam's breakfast – French toast, we want, if you please! – and I've no fire! Where have you *been*?'

Peter only shrugged, and looked gormless. It was

a very useful look, and he was expert at it.

'And what's the matter with you, lurking there in the corner, miss?' Mrs Porter suddenly wheeled round and snapped. 'You look like you've seen a ghost.'

The two young maids, who were drinking tea at the big wooden table, drew in an identical horrified breath, and stared up at Lily.

'Miss Lily, you didn't, did you?' Violet asked, her pale eyes wide.

'Of course she didn't,' Martha murmured, but she was glancing around the darker corners of the kitchen, even so.

'Not a ghost.' Lily shook her head. 'Only Marten. She – she surprised me…' she added, knowing that she sounded foolish.

Mrs Porter made a dismissive noise. 'What would surprise me, Miss Lily, would be if you would keep yourself out of my kitchen for a morning, and stop leading this boy off on some wild goose chase just when I need him.'

'Sorry…' Lily whispered, backing towards the door. Mrs Porter had been scowling down at a spikily written little note lying on the scrubbed wooden table. It was Mama's writing. Lily had been avoiding going anywhere near her mother for weeks, and it seemed that Mama's bad temper was now making itself felt to the servants as well. She was sure that even the air was shimmering slightly, filled with a furious magic that rubbed everyone's nerves raw.

'Oh, stay still, girl!' Mrs Porter shoved an old napkin into her hands, and then snapped at Martha to fill it with some bread and cheese. 'Now, get upstairs, where you belong!'

Lily whisked out of the kitchen without begging for anything else – when Mama was demanding fancy dishes, Mrs Porter had been known to hurl china at Martha, and her aim wasn't good.

'Miss! Miss Lily!' Martha was hissing after her as she hurried through the dark passages away from the servants' quarters. Lily turned back anxiously. 'What is it, Martha? Don't let Mrs Porter catch you. She's in enough of a mood as it is.'

'Here. A mouse wouldn't last on that morsel of bread and cheese.' Martha stuffed a handful of biscuits and an apple into the napkin as well, and kissed Lily's cheek. 'Stay out of the kitchen, you hear? The old dragon's fit to burst. Madam keeps complaining, and Mr Francis disapproved of the rabbit from supper last night.' Martha sniggered. 'He's not even set foot in the kitchen today, he's hiding in the butler's pantry, says he's counting the silver cutlery.'

Lily hugged Martha. 'I won't come near, I promise.

Make sure you duck if she picks up the copper preserving pan, won't you?' She waved to Martha, and hurried away, biting into the apple gratefully. She was making for the orangery, one of the rooms that everyone else at Merrythought House had forgotten about. It had been a beautiful glasshouse once, with a fountain, and a pretty enamel stove to keep the trees warm, but they had all died long ago, and the fountain was blocked up with leaves. It was the perfect place to hide away.

Lily rubbed at a patch of charcoal with her hand, smudging the drawing out. It wasn't good enough. It didn't look real. She sighed, and tucked her knees up under her dirty old dress, hugging them, trying to work out where the drawing had gone wrong. Her dress was filthy, she noticed, and she brushed uselessly at some of the stains on the faded blue and white cotton. But the dirt wasn't just charcoal, it was weeks of wear, and the frock was too short as well. It hardly covered her knees, and the buttons were pulling. She needed a new one, but that would mean asking.

It wasn't the time.

The house was simmering with anger, even more than it had been early in the morning. Lily wasn't sure what was happening, but when she had stolen out of the orangery earlier, she had seen Mama stalking through the passageways, the gold silk of her dress rustling with fury. Mama always walked when she was angry, swishing along like a battleship in full sail. Lily had ducked back down the tiled corridor just in time. It was safer to stay out of Mama's way, and leave her the house to rampage around. Her face had been white, and she was muttering under her breath, words that were so strong Lily could almost see them. She thought of warning Georgiana, but she hadn't seen her sister for weeks. Probably she was in the library. Mama had been coming from that direction, anyway, and Georgiana was almost always shut up in there studying.

Lily allowed herself a moment's resentment of her sister, for being the clever, special one. But it did only last a moment. Over the past few months she had stopped envying Georgiana quite so much. Lily wasn't sure that she wanted all her mother's attention, or even half of it. There were advantages to being the youngest and least interesting; advantages that outweighed too-small dresses and eating in the kitchens.

No lessons, for a start.

Georgiana had lessons all the time, and Lily suspected that Mama's current fury was due to Georgie not doing well enough at them. Georgie was supposed to be a very powerful magician. When she was born, the seer that their parents had brought over to the island had sworn that she was the one, the child all the old magic families were waiting for. The one who would restore the world to the way it should be – with magic no longer outlawed, and the Powers family out of their miserable exile.

Mama hadn't summoned a seer for the inconvenient baby that followed Georgiana. Why would she, when they already had dear little Georgie? Lily was only an afterthought, and no one bothered with her. A slightly smug smile pulled up one corner of Lily's mouth. Being the younger sister of a miracle was easier to bear when the miracle wasn't quite performing as she should.

But then her smile faded. If it was Georgie that had made Mama look like that…

She was hungry, she realised, staring out of the cracked window panes at the high sun. It had to be lunchtime.

She had left the napkin folded up by the draughty French windows which looked out onto the garden, and now she glanced over at it hopefully. She was so hungry that she couldn't possibly have eaten all the bread and cheese… But it was dismally empty, and a small, greyish mouse was just seizing the only crumbs left. It froze for a second as it realised Lily was watching, and then dived for a hole in the crumbling wall.

Lily shuddered. The old orangery was infested with

mice, like the rest of Merrythought House. Mama's cats were far too proud and pampered to chase them, and they scurried everywhere, except the library. Lily was sure that not a single mouse would dare even to poke its whiskers in there.

Another flurry of movement made her catch her breath and swing round in panic. But it wasn't a mouse about to run over her feet. Instead, a tiny brown frog was now sitting in the middle of her charcoal mess, looking doubtful.

Lily smiled to herself. Oddly, although she couldn't stand the mice – she thought it was because of their naked pinkish tails – she found the frogs funny and charming. They had invaded the orangery earlier in the week, a sudden plague of them, and she was rather hoping they would stay.

The confused-looking frog in front of her was actually sitting on a failed drawing of himself – or one of his hundred brothers and sisters. Lily couldn't get the legs right, and it was deeply infuriating. If only she could make them work, the magic would happen again, she was sure.

She had thought she was imagining it at first. Perhaps it had been only a trick of the light, something to do with the fingerish stems of the old vine that was growing out of one of the broken window panes, and colonising the roof. They tapped and wriggled and twisted the sunlight. Lily's charcoal self-portrait – a smudgy picture of a young girl with knotted curly brown hair, and very little nose – had seemed to smile, and half turn her head, as if she were about to say something.

Lily had stared, her heart suddenly squeezing and fluttering inside her. Had that just happened? For a few seconds, the soft charcoal lines had blurred, and thickened, and *moved*, drawing pinkish colour from the cracked terracotta tiles that Lily had been drawing on, and suddenly living.

She had watched it for hours, sitting curled up on the cold floor next to the drawing, until it grew so dark the charcoal lines stole away into the shadows. It hadn't happened again, so perhaps it had only been her imagination. It had seemed so real, though. For a moment, something else had been in the cold, broken room with her. Some*one*.

Ever since, Lily had been waiting for it to happen again, half-hopeful, half-terrified. Did it mean that she was growing magic of her own at last? She was ten, after all, it was the time when it should be happening. Despite her family, her knowledge of magic was only sketchy. She knew fragments of spells, and odd bits of magical theory, but she had only a few old textbooks, and even in those she had skipped the boring bits.

Her favourite was an ancient copy of *Prendergast's Perfect Primer for the Apprentice Magician*, with her father's name, *Peyton Powers*, written in childish handwriting across the flyleaf. It had been jammed upside down in a shelf of books in one of the dustier guest bedrooms in Merrythought, and now Lily treasured it, often tracing her finger over the name and wondering where he was.

She had no memory of him at all. He had been arrested when Lily was only months old for protesting against the Queen's Decree, which outlawed all magic and all magicians. Lily had wondered how one kept a magician in jail, when presumably they could explode chains, and melt walls, and turn guards to stone, but obviously the Queen's Men (it was always said in capitals, like the Decree) had managed it somehow, for her father was in one somewhere on the mainland. She hoped that whatever they used to stop his magic didn't hurt.

One day she might find him. She wasn't entirely sure how, as her mother never left Merrythought, but did that mean she had to stay there for ever, too? And then she might meet other magicians, like the Fells, or the Wetherbys, or the Endicotts, and perhaps someone would teach her, and she would be able to create amazing spells of her own, and learn to fly, and speak to birds, and straighten her stupid curling hair…

But no. There was no magic now. Only hidden away at places like Merrythought, where the ancient magical families pretended they had given it all up, but taught their children the old ways. Or didn't, as the case might be. If Lily left Merrythought and the island, she would never see any magic. She would certainly never be allowed to *do* any, or she'd be thrown into jail.

In any case, according to Mr Prendergast, a ten-year-old magician of any skill should be well up to conversing with magical beasts, and conducting 'simple magical exercises'. Such as making one's name appear written in the air in golden letters of light. And Lily couldn't.

Of course, Georgiana had probably been doing that sort of thing before she was out of her cradle. Now that she was twelve, she had graduated to far more difficult things, which was why Lily never saw her any more. As if it wasn't bad enough just *having* a sister like Georgie, Lily couldn't help loving her as well. Even when she was little, Georgie was always being summoned away by Mama to learn spells, or magical history – which was mostly about how wonderful the Powers family had been before the Decree made any and all magic a crime. But she had always come back eventually. Lily would usually wander down to the kitchen and pester Martha and the other maids while she waited for her sister. It had been in the kitchens that she learned to read, puzzling away at Mrs Porter's stained, precious, handwritten recipe books. If the old cook was in a good mood – which was only when the range was drawing properly; she was always cross when there was an east wind, as it blew back down the chimney and put the fire out – she would let Martha make the fragments of pastry into letters for Lily.

Writing she learned later, when Peter first came. He was only a little older than she was, and the only other child on the island. Naturally Lily wanted to talk to him. But he didn't talk. He didn't listen, either.

He had turned up on the beach, sitting against a rock looking cold and miserable. Martha had found him when she'd gone down to the jetty to pick up the delivery from the grocer on the mainland. The boat with the provisions always came early, before anyone in the house was likely to be up. The money from Merrythought was too good to turn down, but the family were considered strange. Everyone knew what they were, but no one would ever dare say so. Who knew what they might do? Especially her. That ghost-white girl the family were breeding up. She'd been seen, standing on the top of the cliffs, staring out to sea. Looking at the mainland, the fishermen said. What if she were to swim across, like one of those mermaid things that got washed up dead on the shoreline every few years?

Martha still liked to tell the story every so often. How she was walking along, minding her own business – which Lily immediately interpreted as walking along looking for Sam the second footman. Martha was aiming to go up in the world, and she had Sam on a string.

She had been hurrying to fetch the baskets from the jetty, hardly looking at the beach, when out of the corner of her eye, she had seen one of the rocks move. She had thought it was a seal, until it stood up, and she was rooted to the spot, so she said, too shocked even to scream. Lily was sure she'd seen Peter roll his eyes at this, so she suspected that Martha had screamed, quite loudly, the way she had the time a mouse ran over her fingers in the flour-bin.

She had to bring him back to the house, of course. There was nothing else she could do with him. Merrythought was the only house on the island, and everyone in the house had either been born there, or sent from a particularly discreet employment agency. Even Martha and the other maids had signed year-long contracts before they so much as set foot in a boat. They had to promise not to leave, and consent to having all their letters read. Their wages were rather high in consequence.

So Martha had carried one basket back to the kitchen door, and a small, silent child had carried the other.

Lily had been in the kitchen, begging for breakfast, when Martha and the boy turned up. She had gazed at him in amazement – she had, after all, never seen a boy her own age, or any other child but Georgiana.

Mrs Porter looked as though she might fling the dough she was mixing at Martha. 'What on earth is that?' she snapped. 'I sent you to fetch rice, and the pheasants. Am I supposed to roast this scrawny little thing?'

Martha dumped her basket on the kitchen floor and prepared to argue. She was never afraid of Mrs Porter. 'Well, what was I supposed to do, leave him there for the seals to eat? And we've got the groceries, he's carrying half of them!'

'Where did he spring from?' Mr Francis, the butler, was drinking a cup of tea at the table with his waistcoat unbuttoned. He eyed the boy's basket. 'Did they remember the newspapers? She'll be ringing for them, any moment.' He beckoned the boy towards him, right past Lily.

Her eyes were fixed on him as he trailed past, still with his skinny arms wrapped round the basket. Smaller than her, or at least thinner, so thin his cheeks had hollow shadows in them. Dark, spiky hair, and light grey eyes that changed colour, like the sea water he'd appeared from.

'Where did you come from, boy?' Mr Francis asked, peering at him. 'You can put the basket down now.'

The boy said nothing, and didn't put down the basket. He simply stood there.

'He doesn't talk, Mr Francis, I tried,' Martha put in. 'I'm not sure he can hear either.'

The butler frowned, and patted the table, gesturing to the boy to put the basket there. The child did as he was shown, and rubbed his hands over his arms, as if he were cold.

'Well, he's not stupid, even if he can't speak,' Mr Francis muttered. 'We'll have to keep him, I suppose. He hasn't been in the sea, his clothes are dry, and no salt stains, so he hasn't fallen out of a fishing boat.' He shook his head. 'Poor little rat's been abandoned, I should say. Whoever he belongs to didn't want a mute.'

'What do we do with him?' Mrs Porter folded her arms. 'I don't want another child cluttering up my kitchen.'

Lily looked at the cook reproachfully, but then tucked her feet under her chair, to make herself smaller.

'This one you can make wash up. Scrub the floor. Set the mouse traps, whatever you like. No one's going to complain, are they?' Mr Francis shrugged. 'No one else wants him.'

Lily flinched for the boy when Mr Francis said it, but then she realised he was lucky enough not to be able to hear all the things that were said about him.

Mrs Porter sighed expressively. 'Miss Lily, where's that slate Violet found you from the nursery? Let's see if the brat can read.'

Lily fetched the slate from where it was leaning up against the dresser shelf, with the carving platters. Violet, the housemaid, who was just now laying the family's fires upstairs, thought it was shocking that Lily couldn't write. Any village child, she pointed out, would have been dragged to school by an attendance officer by now. She was doing her best to teach Lily in the odd moments she could snatch out of her day, but Lily was slow at it, and slipped out of the kitchens when she heard Violet pattering down the stairs.

Mrs Porter snatched it hurriedly out of her hands – her dough needed time to rise – and scrawled *Name?*, before thrusting it at the boy.

He blinked, and produced a crumpled and raggedy piece of paper from his waistcoat pocket. All it said was *Peter.*

Mrs Porter nodded grimly, and pushed the plate of bread and butter that Martha had been cutting at him.

'He'd better eat something before he gets started,' she muttered, clearly feeling she had to explain her generosity. 'He looks like he might keel over if I ask him to bring the firewood in.'

After that, Lily had been rather more keen on learning to write than before. Her handwriting was nothing like Violet's own delicate copperplate, but it was sufficient to scrawl messages to Peter, inviting him to go and climb the trees in the orchard, or to play ducks and drakes on the beach. It was only rarely that he had time for such games, since everyone in the house gave him all their odd jobs to do, and he couldn't argue back. Often the only way for Lily to be able to borrow him for a game was to do his work for him. By now, she could chop wood, weed a vegetable garden, and polish silver (provided no one was looking, of course). Peter could lip read, when he wanted to, and if people bothered to look straight at him, but notes were still the best way to talk.

Lily sighed, and stared at the blackened mess on the orangery floor, and all over her fingers. Her drawing wasn't much better than her writing, today. She dipped a piece of old rag into a puddle that had leaked through the broken doors, and scrubbed the tiles clean. Then she sat staring at the damp surface for a while, thinking what to draw next. The frogs were impossible, she decided, for they wouldn't sit still long enough for her to get a proper look. And besides, if her drawing should come to life, as her self-portrait had seemed to, did she really need another frog? There were quite enough in the orangery already. There was nothing else in the orangery to copy, so she would have to draw something from memory. She considered another self-portrait, but actually, she didn't want another version of herself either. It would be too odd, and at the same time rather boring. She would much rather have a stranger to talk to.

Lily smiled to herself, as a picture came into her mind. A painting, in fact. One that had hung in the passageway between the drawing room and the library for as long as she could remember. She had always liked the look of the girl – there was something about the way her hair was very smoothly brushed down and bound with ribbons that made Lily suspect it was usually a mad frizz like her own. And the little black pug dog in the girl's arms was clearly on the point of leaping down and running off with the paintbrush.

With her eyes half-closed, Lily began to draw in the girl's face, wishing that she knew her name. She supposed the girl was some sort of relative – perhaps that was why they shared such unruly hair. It was an old painting, though. Lily stared down at the round, amused eyes she had just drawn, and shivered. What if it worked, but the girl appeared as an old, old lady?

Lily sat looking at her stick of charcoal for a few moments, and then sighed, and started to draw the black pug. It wasn't going to work anyway, so it hardly mattered.

The pug was difficult, with all those strange furry wrinkles. She remembered it looking like a little old woman of a dog, apart from those bulgy, sparkling eyes. Lily drew, and smudged away, and drew again, struggling to remember the little face. At last she gave up for a while, and concentrated on the girl's lace-frilled dress. It was very beautiful, pale pink silk. *She must have had dresses like that for every day of the week*, Lily thought, *or she would never have held the dog on her lap in such a beautiful dress*. The black paws had scrumpled up the silk a little, just here, and the polished jet claws would tear it, if the girl wasn't careful.

But the dog's face was still wrong, even if she tried to come at it from the paws, and change the angle. It should be rounder, and almost smiling – why wouldn't it work?

Frustratedly, Lily flung the charcoal down, and leaned back against the wall, scrubbing her eyes with her sleeve. What was the point of crying over it? It was only a charcoal scribble, and it would never be anything else.

Another mouse scrabbled its claws over the tiles, and Lily shuddered, twitching her skirts to scare it away. Her charcoal was pressed back into her hand, and she sighed, wondering whether to carry on and try to get the dog right, or scrub the whole thing out.

Lily gulped. How was she holding the charcoal again? Had it just rolled back into her hand? She stared at the dusty little prints smudging their way across her drawing, and her fingers clenched suddenly around the charcoal stick. It snapped.

Lily looked down, and the dog sitting politely by her knees gazed up at her reproachfully.

Why did I bother to fetch that for you, if all you're going to do is break it? its expression said.

TWO

'It worked,' Lily murmured, staring down at the little black dog. 'It really worked.'

The dog stared back solemnly.

'You are real, aren't you?' Lily whispered, slowly reaching out a hand. The dog watched as she advanced trembling fingers, then darted at her. Lily flinched, then laughed nervously, realising that all the creature had done was lick her. Its tongue was an odd shade of purple – exactly the same as it had been in the painting. Lily had always thought it looked wrong.

'I wonder if your tongue really was that colour...' she whispered. 'Or did I call you back just as you were in the picture?' She frowned. That sort of thing mattered. 'You're a puppy, I think. Not big enough to be a full-grown dog. But does that mean you're a puppy for always?'

The dog turned its head thoughtfully to one side, and then back again, rolling its marble-like eyes. It couldn't have said *No idea* any more clearly.

It stood up, and pattered over to the handkerchief, sniffing it carefully, and then looking as disappointed as Lily had earlier.

'There are lots of mice,' Lily suggested hopefully. 'Wouldn't you like a nice fat mouse?'

The pug's upper lip curled in disgust, and Lily frowned. The dog understood her, she was sure. She supposed it was hardly surprising. Or no more surprising than a dog that had appeared out of a drawing, anyway.

'Maybe not. I wouldn't either, I suppose. I think there are some biscuits in a tin in my room.'

The pug jumped up and ran to the door of the orangery, where it connected back into one of Merrythought's many odd little passageways. It capered around in a circle, waiting for Lily to follow.

'Yes, yes. But you have to hide, you see?' Lily crouched down next to the dancing dog. 'Shh, listen. They won't let me keep you, I'm sure they won't.' Lily blinked. 'Or perhaps it's that I don't want to ask. It doesn't matter. You have to be a secret, do you understand? Quiet?'

The dog nodded solemnly, and Lily laughed. It was such a funny little thing. Then she coughed apologetically, as the huge black eyes took on a look of outrage. She had offended its dignity. She ducked her head. 'I didn't mean to laugh. I'm sorry. This is all – very strange. I mean, I'm talking to a dog. And that's especially odd for me – I don't get to talk to *anyone* a lot of the time. This is the first time I've done magic, too.' Lily shook her head. 'Actually, I didn't really do it. It did itself, it wasn't anything to do with me.' She bent her head down, so she was nose to nose with the pug, its polished fur shining in the evening sun of the orangery. 'Or did you do it?'

The dog looked at her for a second, and then barked. A sharp, demanding little noise, very quick, as though it had remembered Lily's instructions on staying hidden.

'Hurry up with the food?' Lily asked, standing up, and the little dog skittered around her feet joyfully. 'Stay close then. And you might have to hide.'

There was a streak of black, as the dog shot back across the orangery to seize the empty napkin, and trotted back with the cloth trailing like a banner across its back.

'Oh! Good idea.' Lily bent down to take it, and

gasped as the dog sprang into her arms, and then licked her cheek affectionately. It sat up high in her arms, riding like royalty – it was a look Lily remembered from the painting. Carefully, she draped the napkin around the dog's head. 'Just duck down, if anyone comes,' she murmured, slipping out into the passageway.

But they didn't meet anyone as they moved swiftly through the house. It was early evening. Mama would be resting, and the servants would take the chance to rest too, gathered in the kitchens, getting under Mrs Porter's feet.

Lily stopped in the passage between the drawing room and the library, eyeing the library door anxiously. She was almost sure Mama was upstairs, but one never knew… There wasn't a sound. Breathing a little more easily, she scurried to the gilt frame of the painting she wanted, and looked up curiously. In her arms, the dog looked up too.

The girl was still there, but she had no pretty little black dog. Instead she held a flower in her hands, gripping the stem remarkably tightly. Almost as though she were twisting it between her fingers. Her pretty painted smile was practically a grimace, Lily noticed. And there was just the faintest little dark smear on her pink silk skirts – a tiny muddy paw mark.

'I didn't mean to steal you,' Lily whispered guiltily

to the dog. 'She looks *furious*.'

The dog wriggled forward a little, and placed its claws on the gilt frame, sniffing at the canvas. Then it tried a delicate lick, its head on one side in that curious pose again. Then it snuggled back into Lily's arms, in a way that suggested it much preferred being where it was now.

Lily laughed quietly to herself, as the dog's solid little body nuzzled up against her. She could feel the muscles moving under the smooth pelt of black fur as it wriggled. The dog didn't feel like a spell, or a ghost, or something she'd imagined. The solid warmth against her chest was comfortingly real.

There was the faintest rustle behind the library door, and Lily jumped, and turned in one quick movement to race for the stairs. No one came after her.

She was still looking back down into the hall, wondering if her mother had somehow learned what she had done – surely the others in the house would notice the furious little girl in the painting? So when she brushed against someone on the stairs, she cried out in surprise, and flung herself back against the wall. The dog had had the sense to duck under the napkin, but a coal-black nose was still poking out, sniffing with interest at this new person.

Luckily, the girl on the stairs hardly seemed to notice.

She simply glanced dismally at Lily, and turned to carry on down into the hallway.

Crossly, Lily stuck out her tongue at her sister, and hissed, making the dog prick up its tiny ears. Georgiana might at least say something. Obviously she was too grand and important to talk to her little sister now.

Georgiana turned round and looked back up at Lily. It was hard to see in the gloom of the dark-painted stairwell, but Lily took a step back in surprise, almost falling up the stairs. Georgie looked like a ghost. Her white-blonde hair was straw-like, and her pale skin had faded to a greyish, unhealthy tint. It made the red rims around her eyes stand out even more.

'Are you crying?' Lily asked her curiously, feeling half-guilty. What did Georgie have to cry for?

Her sister made a strange hiccupping noise, and ran back up the stairs, her skirts brushing against Lily and the dog as she swept past. Lily heard her race along the passage, and fumble with her door, finally slamming it behind her.

'What's the matter with her?' Lily muttered crossly. It was the first time she had seen Georgie in days. Now she couldn't even feel properly indignant about her sister ignoring her any more, she was going to have to worry about her instead.

'I don't know. Who was she?' a muffled voice asked

from under the napkin. The black pug shook itself, emerging out of the folds of fabric with an air of relief. 'She smelled nice.'

Lily's eyes widened, so that they were almost, but not quite, as round as the pug's.

'What?' the dog asked, twitching its eyes from side to side irritably. 'I know this cloth looks stupid. You told me to hide. I was trying my best. The other girl didn't see me, I don't think, but then I suppose she wasn't in much of a state to notice anything, was she?'

Lily shook her head dumbly.

The dog put its head on one side again. 'Ah. Were you not expecting me to talk?'

'No...' Lily whispered. 'To be honest, I wasn't expecting you at all.'

'But you asked me!' the dog protested. 'Not that I'm not grateful. I don't really remember being stuck in that painting, but it can't have been very exciting. You called me here.' It eyed her doubtfully. 'I do hope you're not going to send me back?'

'Oh, no, no!' Lily shook her head, and unconsciously tightened her hold on the dog. 'Please don't go. I wanted someone to come, although I did think it might be your mistress, the girl in the pink silk dress. I thought she looked interesting, and I was desperate for someone to talk to. I'm just honestly surprised that anyone came at all. I didn't expect it to work.' She frowned down at the dog. 'Where did you actually come from? I mean, how did I get you here?'

The dog shrugged. 'You're the one who's supposed to know that, I'm afraid. It was something I couldn't help doing. Like chasing a ball. And the talking is new, I ought to add, I don't think I could do it before. It's your fault, I think. You wanted someone who would talk back.'

'But…what are you?'

The dog gazed up at her, its wrinkled little face giving it a look of amusement. 'I'm a *dog*.'

'Yes, but—'

The dog shrugged. 'You'll have to be satisfied with that. It's all I can tell you. Now, biscuits? And while we're finding them, who is the other girl? The one who looks like a miserable mouse?'

Lily stumbled up the stairs, too intent on staring at the dog to look where she was going. 'That's my sister. Georgiana. I don't see her very much.'

'Whyever not? Arabel – my mistress, the pink-dress girl – she had three sisters, and we could never get away from them.'

'Arabel…' Lily murmured. 'Georgie told me about her. She was one of our great-aunts. She made weather spells, and she never ever wore coats. Weather spells are supposed to be a Powers thing, we're all meant to be good at them.'

The dog sniffed. 'After my time, I think. Arabel's spells always went wrong, when I knew her. Why don't you see your sister?'

'She's too busy. She's being taught, you see. She's supposed to revive the fortunes of the family, so things can go back to the way they were before.'

'Before what?'

Lily stopped at the top of the stairs. 'Oh! Of course, you wouldn't know. Before the Decree. Um…magic isn't allowed any more.'

The dog stared at her, and then snorted dismissively. 'Who says?'

'Queen Sophia ordered it – after a magician called Marius Grange killed her father, King Albert. Thirty years ago.'

'Did she now…?' the dog said slowly. 'Well, that would do it. Completely banned?'

Lily nodded. 'Completely. For ever. That's why Mama is secretly teaching Georgie, and Father is in prison. And why we never leave the island.'

The dog shook its whiskers in a sort of shudder. 'You don't go to the London house, even?'

'We don't have it any more. We lost a lot of money after the Decree, and the London house was taken away.

Stolen, Georgie used to say. Then Father tried to have an audience with the queen, to persuade her that not all magicians were mad. Only it went terribly wrong, somehow, and he was thrown into prison. There's some money, from Mama's family, just not as much of it as there used to be. Mama complains that we're beggars now, but Martha – she's one of the maids – says that's complete nonsense, and Mama hasn't a clue. Beggars don't have maids, for a start, she says.' Lily paused, and then asked hesitantly, as though she felt she should already know, 'Do you have a name? I can't just call you Dog.'

The pug dipped its head a little shyly, and nodded. 'Henrietta. Arabel chose it.' It glanced up at her, seeming uncertain for the first time.

Lily smiled. It was a strange, fussy-sounding name, but it suited the odd little creature. 'It's pretty,' she promised. Then she sighed. 'Do you think I should talk to Georgie?'

Henrietta nodded vigorously. 'Yes. I want to know what she's looking so woebegone about.' She looked up at Lily. 'I like knowing things, and it's most unpleasant not knowing anything after years being shut up in a frame. Everything seems to have changed.' She glanced sideways at the faded, gently peeling wallpaper. 'And not necessarily for the better. I need to find some things out.'

'So you couldn't ever see anything when you were in the painting?' Lily asked curiously. 'You weren't – alive?'

Henrietta frowned. The wrinkles on her face deepened, enough for Lily to think idly that they were deep enough to hide marbles in. 'Just occasionally. I think it was if someone with a lot of magic stood near, and actually *saw* us, really looked, I mean. Then I could see too.' She nudged Lily's cheek with her startlingly cold nose. 'I saw you.'

Lily blushed. 'I liked looking at you, and Great Aunt Arabel. I always wished you'd come out of the picture. But I'm not the one with a lot of magic, that's Georgie.'

Henrietta shrugged. 'You've got enough. Is this her room?'

Lily nodded, and knocked on the door. There was an intent, listening silence from inside, but that was all. She tried the handle, but the door seemed to be locked – which was odd, because she knew that the key had been lost years ago. Still, she supposed Georgie didn't need a key to lock her door any more. She stroked the door panels thoughtfully, wondering what spell her sister had used. Until an hour or so before, she would have stomped away grumpily, shut out by magic again. But now she had Henrietta. She didn't know quite what that proved, but she was sure it was something. Could she feel a prickle in her fingertips as she swept them across the edge of the door? Perhaps.

'I can't make it open,' she whispered to Henrietta. 'But I've an idea.'

Lily hurried along the passage to her own door, which was next to Georgie's, and slipped inside. She had left the window open that morning, as the clear richness of the blue sky had promised another hot day.

Henrietta looked around curiously as Lily put her down on the chair by the tall window. 'This is a nice room. Arabel slept on the other side of the house, I think. This must look out on the rose garden – over the blue drawing room, yes? It's rather dusty though.' She sneezed delicately.

Lily sighed. 'It's hard to get maids who want to come and live on the island. They have to sign a paper saying they'll stay, you see. Most girls won't. They know something strange must be happening here, something wrong, so they don't want to work here.'

Henrietta nodded thoughtfully. 'Do your servants know about the magic, then?'

Lily shrugged. 'Everyone knows, but they never say. Not once they've met Mama, anyway. Who would dare? When the Queen's Men come and question the servants to make sure that we're all keeping to the terms of the Decree, Mama is always standing behind them, with her

arms folded, and that look she has. They'd never tell.'
She smiled. 'And they have to be very well paid, which is
another reason we don't have enough maids to clean my
bedroom very often.' She glanced around. 'I suppose it
is dirty. I do try and dust it sometimes.'

'I want to see your sister again.' The black dog
jumped down from the chair and followed her to the
window. 'You said you had an idea?'

'Oh, yes. Look, out here. There's a balcony, and
Georgie's room has one too. It isn't far from one to the
other.' Lily stepped over the low sill of the window, and
leaned over to look along the wall. 'Georgie's window is
open too!' she hissed.

Henrietta put her paws on the windowsill and peered
out. 'That may not be far for you, Lily, but I think I shall
stay here. Pugs aren't built for climbing. I shall watch. If
you can persuade your sister to open her door, then you
can come and let me in.' Then her ears twitched, and
when she spoke again it was in a lower voice, not her
usual ladylike growly squeak. 'I can hear someone.
Downstairs.'

Lily, who had been hanging over the delicate
wrought-iron balcony, trying to see into Georgie's room,
gave a little gasp. 'Mama uses the blue drawing room,'
she whispered.

'Someone else too. She's talking to someone. Shhh,

listen.' The little dog settled her chin on her front paws with a gleeful expression. Clearly the occupants of the room below had moved closer to the open French windows. Lily sat down on the balcony, leaning against the railings, and hearing the words drift out into the summer evening.

'Is she any better, ma'am?'

'She's talking to Marten, her lady's maid,' Lily whispered.

'Hardly at all. I had such hopes…' There was a rustle of stiff silk that made Lily shiver. Mama was pacing again, her skirt swishing around her.

'Are they talking about your sister?' Henrietta breathed.

'I expect so.'

There was silence for a moment from downstairs, then as Lily's mother came past the window again, her voice floated upwards, unnaturally clear. 'If only I could do it myself…'

Lily shivered. Mama was speaking half-spells again, the words forming strange colours and lights in Lily's mind, like swirls of scented smoke. She shook them away hastily, digging the hard iron of the balcony rail into her hands, until her mind was clear again.

'But the prophecy was quite clear. It has to be a child that brings it all about. I was so certain that she was the one. That seer I brought over here after she was born swore to me that this was the child that had been foretold. She lied, perhaps… Well, I suppose we can always send this one the way of the others. But such a lot of time wasted!' An expressive sigh. 'And I am running out of time…' She laughed bitterly. 'And children.'

Lily frowned at Henrietta, whose ears were twitching frantically. 'What does that mean? Oh, there's the bell, and I can hear her moving away. She's going in to dinner.'

'Look!' the pug hissed, nodding towards the next-door balcony. 'How long has she been there?'

Lily twisted round, gripping the railings and looking across at Georgie's balcony. It was wider than her own, and she hadn't noticed the strange little heap in the corner when she was trying to look into Georgie's room. But now she realised that it was Georgie herself, curled up against the wall, her whitish hair shining in the strange thundery evening light. Listening.

'Georgie! Mama and Marten have gone. Georgie, I want to talk to you. Unlock your door, please! I'm sorry I was mean.'

But her sister didn't so much as move.

'Oh!' Lily muttered crossly. 'Well, I shall just have to climb across and shake her! I'll make her listen!' She sprang up, and swung one leg over the low iron railings.

'Be careful…' Henrietta laid her ears back. 'The whole house is crumbling, that doesn't look at all safe – and where are you going to put that foot now? Not there, you can't reach! Lily, no!'

But Lily had jumped, flinging herself at the next balcony, the same way she clambered about in the apple trees in the orchard. Except there she fell onto long grass and several years' worth of rotten apples, not a stone flagged terrace.

With one elbow hooked around the top edge of Georgie's balcony, Lily heaved to pull herself up, but she could feel her arm slipping already.

'Georgie, help me!' she gasped, her breath coming in frightened pants. But her sister seemed far away, her eyes blank and staring behind a white veil of hair.

Henrietta had scrambled out of the window, and was now scurrying backwards and forwards on the balcony, whining in horror. Then all at once she barked, a sharp, angry noise, that caught the back of Lily's neck like nails scratching down paint. She shuddered horribly, and managed to struggle another couple of inches of arm over the railings.

Georgie stirred for the first time, flinging her hair back out of her face wearily, like someone waking from a strange dream.

'Lily!'

THREE

'What were you doing, you idiot?' Georgie yelled, hauling her little sister over onto her balcony.

Lily sat panting on the stone floor, rubbing her strained arms, and giggling feebly.

'Don't *laugh!*' Georgie snapped, giving her a little shake. 'What were you thinking of? You would have died if you'd fallen onto the terrace!'

'I know. But it's so funny – this is the first time you've acted like my big sister in ages. Maybe I should do stupid things more often.' She smiled up at Georgie, leaning back against her sister's knees, and not minding the tight grip of her fingers. 'Wouldn't you have cast a spell to catch me, anyway, if I fell?'

Her sister sat down next to her, hugging her arms

around her knees. 'I don't know if I could, Lily.' She closed her eyes, as though it hurt to look at her sister. 'I would have tried. Of course I would. But nothing works.'

'The prophecy…' Lily started.

'Wrong.' Georgie shrugged. 'Or perhaps that seer was simply too frightened of Mama to say anything different. Mama's worried that another child will be better than I am. There are other magical families still. There's an Endicott girl, the same age as me, she says…'

'Oh…' Lily nodded thoughtfully. 'So that's why Mama is so angry all the time now.' Then she frowned. 'Georgie, what is it that they want you to do?'

There was a skitter of claws, and Henrietta poked her wrinkled muzzle through the bars of Lily's balcony. 'Yes! I want to know that too, please!'

Georgie sprang up, nearly tipping Lily over, then seized her sister, and dragged her back against the wall of the house, holding an arm across her front. 'Who's there?' she snapped.

'Georgie, stop it!' Lily wriggled out from Georgie's grip, and pointed. 'Look! It's only Henrietta.' She smiled, a proud little smirk. 'She's my dog. I brought her out of the picture of the girl in the pink silk dress downstairs. It's Great Aunt Arabel, did you know that?' She looked up, and caught the expression of horror and fear that had turned Georgie even paler than she was before. 'What is it? Oh… Are you worried that I stole her? Great Aunt Arabel does look rather cross about it, but unless we bring her out of the picture too, there isn't a great deal she can do, is there? Don't worry, Georgie.'

But her sister was staring at her, her eyes dark violet pools in her white face, eyes the colour of bruises. '*You* brought the little dog out of the painting? Your magic – you're starting to find your magic,' she murmured, her face twisting strangely.

Lily nodded. 'Are you angry?' she asked, her voice small and thin. 'I won't tell Mama, if you don't want me to. I'm sure yours will work again – perhaps it's – it's just your age…'

'Oh, Lily…' Georgie murmured. Then she laughed. 'That pug is going to have a fit if we leave her there much longer.'

Henrietta whined crossly. 'I shall stick here if I put my head any further through these bars,' she pointed out. 'You are most unkind, talking so quietly, and on the other balcony. Come back here!' She wriggled herself back out of the bars with an almost audible pop.

'Come back to my room?' Lily pleaded. 'We could curl up on my bed. We haven't done that for so long. Please, Georgie.'

Georgie nodded, stepping back in through her

window, and holding her hand out to Lily to follow her.

Lily looked around curiously as her sister crept to the door. Georgie's room had changed in the last year or so, since she had last been allowed to play in there with her sister. The pretty furniture was pushed out of the way, leaving room for swaying towers of books and papers. Odd vessels were dotted here and there, most of them with strange crusts of old spells staining the glass, as though Georgie had been desperately practising between her lessons. Georgie hardly seemed to notice, simply weaving her way between the piles to the door. Lily caught her breath as she saw that there was a scarlet thread tied around the white porcelain door handle, but Georgie untangled it so easily, how could it be a spell? Then the door swung open as soon as she pulled the thread away, and Lily caught her arm.

'You see, you can still do some things!'

Georgie shrugged. 'It's just a trick – a silly little charm. Anyone could do it, if they were taught. You too, now, Lily.' She shook her head, her eyes stricken again. 'Come on, we have to talk. I'm so stupid, I should have thought it all out properly before.'

'What?' Lily murmured, following Georgie along the passage to her own room. Her sister pushed her inside, and leaned against the door for a second, as though she finally felt safe. Then she ran her fingertips around the door frame, hauling over a stool so she could reach to the very top. The dim line of shadow around the door glowed silvery for a second as she did it, and then it was just a door again.

'Silence spell,' Georgie muttered. 'Shut the window. Oh!' In spite of herself she sputtered with laughter as she saw Henrietta bound and scrabble back over the windowsill.

The little black dog landed in a clumsy tangle of paws, but then she stood up, and stalked delicately across the room to Lily, glaring at Georgie with her enormous eyes. 'You look a sight,' she pointed out, disapprovingly. 'Your hair is dirty.'

Georgie stroked one hand down her lank blonde hair, flushed pink, and nodded. 'I haven't had time…' she murmured.

Henrietta snorted. 'What exactly is it they're making you do, that gives you no time to wash?'

Georgie frowned. 'I don't know, exactly… I think Mama put some sort of…binding on me. Most of the time, I hardly think of anything except work – practising spells, over and over, trying to make them perfect. I don't seem to care about anything else.' She shivered. 'Sometimes it's as though I'm watching myself, as if I were floating on the ceiling, looking down, and then I just think, *Poor Georgie… Still not good enough.*

I think she's getting desperate. I should be better. Perhaps she thought you were distracting me from working.' She rubbed a hand over her eyes, wearily. 'I'm not sure how long it's been that way.'

Lily frowned. 'I've hardly seen you since last summer, Georgie. That's when Mama started teaching you all the time, not just in the mornings. It was like you lived in the library, all of a sudden. When did you last go outside?'

Georgie shook her head, looking dazed.

'And if I did see you, it would be like today on the stairs – you'd just brush past me, as if I didn't exist.'

'Last summer?' Georgie whispered. The pink faded suddenly out of her cheeks. She was so pale now that the red rims around her eyes were startling. 'Then it's been a whole year, and I haven't improved at all. And I hardly remember any of it…' She swayed on her feet, and Lily hauled her across the room to the bed, forcing her to sit down. Henrietta jumped up, scratching at the bedcovers and glaring, until Lily lifted her up too. Then she padded over to Georgie, and sat down with her paws in the girl's lap, staring up at her anxiously.

'What happened today to make you see your sister?' she demanded.

Georgie shook her head slowly. 'I don't know. She was there, on the stairs. Nothing seemed different – I was surprised to see her, I thought how long it was since we'd talked. But I was supposed to go and find a book, one that I'd left downstairs. And then she hissed at me…'

Lily's tightened her arm around her sister's shoulder. 'I was cross. I'm sorry, I didn't mean to upset you – or not very much…'

Henrietta shook her ears briskly. 'Don't apologise to her, Lily. You broke her out of a spell. She should be thanking *you*.'

Georgie wound her fingers in her hair, pulling it so tightly that it had to hurt. 'It must be because your own magic's working now. That's why I saw you all of a sudden, and you broke Mama's binding.'

Henrietta flashed her startlingly white teeth. 'She's had a busy day.'

'You have to hide it!' Georgie suddenly twisted round to grab at Lily, making her gasp and pull back, wriggling away and squirming into the pillows. She'd never seen Georgie look so strange. Her eyes had darkened so that they were almost black now.

Henrietta had backed away, growling on a low, disturbing note, her paws catching on the bedcovers.

'Why?' Lily faltered. Was Georgie jealous? Lily swallowed tears. She'd hoped her big sister would be proud of her. Ever since Georgie had stopped talking to her, Lily had told herself that she hated her sister.

Georgie had abandoned her, after all. But secretly – so secretly she hadn't even known it herself – she had wanted to show Georgie that she could be special too.

Georgie let go of her, sighing. 'I frightened you.' She smoothed Lily's crumpled sleeve apologetically. 'Lily, don't you see? I've always done what she's told me. I went along with it, like a good, dutiful daughter. I wouldn't dare do anything else. But until you asked me, I've never thought about *why*. Or what I'm actually supposed to do! And that's just stupid.' She laughed. 'I can tell you think so. You're both trying not to look disgusted, but the dog isn't very good at keeping a straight face.'

Lily glanced down at Henrietta, who did indeed look very disapproving. She could tell that the pug wanted to leap up and down, and pound Georgie with questions – just as she did.

'You really don't know what it is she's training you for?' she asked, her voice a little disbelieving. 'But you always told me… About how terrible the queen is, and that the Decree was wrong, and one day all the magicians will stand together and prove it. You're the one who's going to put everything back the way it should be.'

Georgie nodded. 'I only told you that because it's what Mama told me! She's been telling me it for ever, Lily! Since I was too little to read a book of spells, even.

It's always the prophecy, and my destiny, and our heritage. But what does that mean? How am I actually supposed to *do* it?'

'Why haven't you just asked her?' Henrietta demanded. Her wrinkles were still arranged in a disapproving stare.

Georgie took a breath, as though she was about to speak, but then she sighed, sinking her chin in her hands, and staring down at the bedspread. When she looked up at last, her eyes were their usual blue, but her face was still distinctly miserable. 'I suppose partly I was scared to. But I think the binding spell stopped me asking that too. She doesn't want me to know. So it must be something awful.'

'What sort of thing?' Lily frowned. 'I always thought it meant you were going to be so good at magic that no one could stop you doing it, and you'd be able to persuade the queen that magic was a good thing. All the magicians would be allowed to come out of hiding at last, and you would lead them. Father would be pardoned, and everyone would be happy again...' Lily was smiling as she said it, her voice slow and dreamy. It was her favourite daydream, after all. But then she trailed off, realising how silly the words sounded in a dark, grubby room, with her frightened sister and a talking dog.

Henrietta sniffed. 'That sounds like a fairy tale to me.'

Lily swallowed, feeling her fantasy world slip away. 'I suppose it isn't very likely, after all... But Mama's always said Georgie would save us. How else is she going to do it? Especially if she doesn't even know what she's doing.'

There was silence in the bedroom, as everyone considered this, worriedly.

'Perhaps Mama doesn't know how you're going to do it either?' Lily suggested. 'Maybe she's just hoping that if she trains you well enough, you'll manage somehow.'

Georgie shook her head. 'No, from the way she talks about it, I'm sure there's something particular she wants me to do. Something strange, and – and dangerous.' She frowned. 'I just remember little glimpses. Odd words. But I can't put them all together, even now Lily's undone me.'

Lily giggled. It sounded like she'd unlaced Georgie's petticoats. But the urge to laugh didn't last long. 'Will Mama be able to tell I've done it?' she asked suddenly, her heart thudding into a frightened little rush. 'When you have another lesson, will she see her spell has gone? What will she say?'

Georgie nibbled the end of her hair, despite Henrietta's disapproving growl. 'I have to, it helps me to think!' At last she shook her head. 'I don't think so, Lily. Not if I'm careful to act the way I always do, and not ask any questions.' She smiled, but not happily. 'Most of the time Mama is so angry with me, she wouldn't notice if I turned blue. And if she does notice, Lily, I won't tell her you've done it. She mustn't know. You must keep your magic a secret, I'm certain of it. Perhaps that was partly what woke me out of the spell? Knowing that I had to protect you?'

'I approve of secrets, generally,' Henrietta announced, 'provided *I* know them, of course. But why is it so important that Lily hides her magic?'

Georgie sighed. 'My magic isn't working the way it's supposed to. Mama's furious. Don't you see? If I'm no good, Lily, they'll take you instead.'

Lily nodded slowly. She felt strangely torn inside. It was what she'd always wanted – to be as special and important as Georgie. But suddenly it seemed better to stay ordinary.

'Moving on to the next one...' Henrietta said thoughtfully. She lay down on the bed, stretching her paws out in front of her like a little Chinese lion. Lily lay down next to her, propping herself on her elbows to look at her sister, curled on the other side of the dog.

'It isn't as if I'm the first,' Georgie murmured, stroking Henrietta's soft black head.

Lily stared at her. 'What do you mean?'

Georgie blinked, and shook her head, almost as if she were shaking something loose. 'Something Mama said, I think. Since the spell's gone, odd wisps of things just keep swirling around in my head. She's angry because she's done this all before.'

Lily wriggled upright again, her words falling all over each other in her excitement. 'Yes! Yes, she said so. Just now, to Marten, don't you remember? She said something about *the others*.' She shivered, and put her hand on Henrietta's back for comfort. The little dog shuddered and half snapped, as though Lily's fingers were icy. 'In the chapel, Georgie. The stones, with the names. Lucy. And – and…'

'Prudence,' Georgie added in a whisper. 'But they were babies.'

'There aren't any dates on the stones, Georgie.'

'Wouldn't you remember them, if they were old enough to be learning magic, when they…went?' Henrietta asked.

Georgie shook her head. 'The stones have been there as long as I can remember. Perhaps Mama was very young when she had them? Oh, this is stupid – we're making it up out of nothing. She was young, and they died. They're just babies who died, Lily, that's all. It happens all the time!'

Lily nodded gratefully. Just now, she would have given anything to believe that Georgie was right. All she wanted to do was curl up and lie next to her sister, and pet the dog, and not have to think. But her thoughts were betraying her, whirling around free and refusing to be called back.

The sweet, soft-furred little dog was the result of a spell. Her magic was growing inside her, and sooner or later, her mother was going to find out.

However much Georgie had disappointed Mama, her sister's skin still hummed with magic when Lily touched her. She could feel it now, shimmering between them. There was something inside her, some strange, dangerous magic, underlain with Georgie's own gentler power.

Lily couldn't hide away in the orangery any longer.

FOUR

'Ahem!'

Lily jumped, as a chill nose nudged her wrist. 'What is it?'

Henrietta sighed, and even though Lily had known her only a few hours, it was clear that this was the sigh of a put-upon dog.

'You mentioned biscuits?'

'Sorry...' Lily sat up, and rummaged on the little table beside her bed for matches to light the oil lamp. Then she pulled out the tarnished old silver biscuit barrel.

Henrietta stood up eagerly, her tail whirring from side to side, as it was too tightly curled to wag like any other dog's. 'Oh, with raisins! I adore raisins.' She took the biscuit Lily gave her delicately in her teeth, and crunched it happily, then licked the bedcover to clear up any crumbs. Then she sat hopefully in front of Lily, staring up at her, huge eyes shining with love and starvation.

'Another one?' Lily suggested, holding a biscuit above the little black nose, and giggling.

'I haven't been fed for about sixty years,' Henrietta pointed out plaintively. 'I am *very* hungry.' She jumped on all four feet at once, and seized the biscuit from Lily's fingers. 'Hah! You didn't know I could do that, did you?' she asked Lily, smugly, through crumbs.

By the time Henrietta had had four biscuits, and Lily and Georgie two each, the tin was empty, even Henrietta admitting this at last, after snuffling around inside it quite thoroughly for a while. She sighed heavily, and settled back down on the bedcover, yawning, and licking her jowls, in case she had missed any crumbs. Then she looked up at Lily and Georgie, bright-eyed.

'So what are we going to do?'

Georgie stared at her. 'Do…?' she faltered.

'We have to do something,' Lily pointed out gently. 'At the very least, we have to find out what Mama is planning. It's your life, Georgie! You can't just let her use you in some strange plot.'

Henrietta shook her head briskly. 'No. You should

definitely know what the plot is first. Very irresponsible not to.'

Georgie closed her eyes, wearily. 'I almost wish I'd walked on down the stairs,' she murmured. 'Oh, not really. It was just so much easier to let Mama order me around. You're terribly bossy, Lily. And the dog is worse...'

'*The dog* is a very rude thing to say,' Henrietta said sniffily. 'I have a name.'

'You see – you sound like a fussy governess!' Georgie shook her head. 'But I know you're right,' she added, staring miserably at her fingers. 'I just don't want to.'

Henrietta padded across the coverlet to Lily, and snuffled in her ear. 'Have you ever noticed that your sister is awfully *wet*?'

'So would you be if you were under a spell the whole time and never allowed to do anything but work,' Lily said defensively. But she couldn't help agreeing a little.

'It's probably why she's no good at this spell-plot thing,' Henrietta added, in a loud and indiscreet whisper. 'She's just not got the guts for it.'

'That isn't fair!' Lily snapped, sounding even crosser because she had a horrible feeling Henrietta was right.

'It's true, Lily.' Georgie glanced up, and she was laughing. 'Maybe you should show Mama your magic.

You'd be far better at it. Although I'm not sure her binding spell would work on you, you'd probably throw it back in her face. You're very like her, actually. Determined.'

'I just want to know what's happening,' Lily said stubbornly. 'And if you can't ask – well, then we need to find out somehow. Some other way.'

Georgie put her hair in her mouth again, a whole hank of it, and nibbled it fast. Chewing on her hair she seemed more mouse-like than ever, and Lily eyed her worriedly. Much as she hated for Henrietta to be right, Georgie didn't look like much of a co-conspirator. She looked like a frightened twelve-year-old, who might fall over if someone spoke too loudly.

'How?' she murmured, through her hair.

'I suppose when you're in the library, Mama is usually watching you…' Lily began thoughtfully. 'So you wouldn't be able to look around for – for evidence. We need to get in there another time.'

Georgie drew her knees up to her chest, and wrapped her arms around them. Her thin little wrists poked out of her lacy sleeves, and she was shivering. 'Must we?'

Henrietta snorted – although in a very ladylike manner. 'Wet!' she whispered to Lily again.

Lily tried to put a finger over Henrietta's mouth, and then gasped with laughter as she met cold wet nose instead. Henrietta leaned against her lovingly. '*I* will come and help you look.'

Georgie looked up, her blue eyes hardening, so they reminded Lily of the smoky blue-grey flints she found on the beach sometimes. She glared at Henrietta. 'And so will I. You've never met our mother, remember. You don't know what you're promising to do.'

Henrietta sniffed, but she did shift her hindquarters a little nervously, as though Georgie's words went home.

'We'll have to watch for when Mama leaves the library,' Lily mused, and Georgie nodded unwillingly. 'I suppose we could go hunting then.'

'Good. So tomorrow, you have to be just as you always are,' Lily told her sister firmly.

Georgie gulped, and Lily eyed her with frustration. 'You *have* to!'

'I will!' Georgie snapped back. 'You don't know what it's like, sitting there in the library trying to learn spells with Mama watching me all the time. And now I'll be worrying that she can see her spell's gone. I shall spend the whole time certain that she's standing just behind me, with her fingers outstretched...' She shuddered fitfully, having succeeded in frightening herself and Lily, and even Henrietta, whose eyes were bulging more than usual.

Lily swallowed. 'I know. I mean, I know that I *don't*

know. I want to help, Georgie. You can't want to be sitting there like that for the rest of your life.'

'It wouldn't be...' Georgie began, but her voice trailed away to a whisper. 'I suppose it could.'

'Especially if your life wasn't very long,' Henrietta pointed out helpfully.

Lily glared at her. 'Are all dogs tactless, or is it only you?' she hissed.

Henrietta shrugged, and stretched out her paws. 'Dogs are not tactless. We just don't see the point in polite little lies. Which is all tact is, you know.'

Lily opened her mouth to argue, and then shut it again. Henrietta seemed to be right.

'I'm going to sneeze,' Henrietta muttered dolefully in Lily's ear.

'You mustn't!'

'Your housekeeper is worse than useless. The dust!'

'We don't have one any more,' Lily murmured, peering round the heavy, dusty, velvet curtain at the library door. 'Only a butler, Mr Francis, and he's a little shortsighted.'

'Miss Arabel's mother would have sacked half the staff if they'd let the house get into this state. *Grr.*' The pug dog shook her head, pawing at her nose miserably.

'You do know we're supposed to be hiding?' Lily pointed out. 'Shh!'

Henrietta peeped round the curtain. 'Oh, no one can hear us, Lily! That's a big solid door. I really don't see why we have to lurk here anyway. Can't your sister just come and tell us when your mother has gone?'

Lily sighed, and huddled herself back onto the wide windowsill behind the curtain. 'Yes… Except – I'm not absolutely sure she would.' She could imagine Georgie in the library, shivering, trying to nerve herself to get up and fetch them. It was safer to watch themselves.

Henrietta nudged her gently, and then reared up on her hind paws to look out of the smeared window glass. 'I can see the sea from here. Lily, have you really never been off this island?'

'Never.'

Henrietta shuddered. 'I am a London dog. The countryside is all very well, but I like pavement under my paws. I suppose London has changed too,' she muttered, sounding quite indignant about it. Then she whisked round on the windowsill, her ears suddenly pricked. 'Someone is coming!'

'Perhaps she's going upstairs at last.' Lily squidged herself as far back into the window as she could.

'No, no.' Henrietta was quivering excitedly. 'The other way! Someone is coming down the stairs.'

'Oh!' Lily frowned. 'I suppose it must be one of the maids, Martha or Violet. But we've been here ages, and I didn't see anyone go up.'

'Someone very small. Or perhaps just light. And odd-smelling. Ugh. No, a horrible smell. Sour and wrong and...not good! Who is this, Lily? No, shh, be quiet, she's coming through the hall.'

Light feet were tapping across the stone floor of the hall, and making for the passage they were hiding in. Together, Lily and Henrietta spied around the curtain as a woman in a black dress, swathed in a veil, pattered past them, knocked quietly at the door of the library, and disappeared inside.

'So? Who was she?' Henrietta leaned out after her as the door slammed.

'It's Marten. Mama's lady's maid. She *is* horrible.' Lily shivered. 'Sort of shadowy... But she doesn't smell, or at least, I never thought she did. She always looks scrubbed. Her dress is spotless. The Talish are very good at ironing, I think.'

Henrietta eyed her pityingly. 'She smells. Believe me. But it isn't anything to do with not washing. I shouldn't think she needs to wash, that one.' There was a curious glint in her black eyes. 'Why do you not like her, then?'

Lily frowned. 'Well... She never speaks to me. Most of the rest of the servants do. They – they pity me,

I think. Martha's always slipping me extra food, and Violet tries to teach me my letters. They know I don't have any magic,' – she ignored Henrietta snorting – 'and they think I'm neglected.'

'You *are* neglected. Thank goodness. If you were being taught like your sister, you'd never have had the time to find me.'

'The really strange thing about Marten is her eyes,' Lily added suddenly. 'She has awful eyes. They're grey, and they don't have any middle. The pupils. She doesn't have them. Or the whites. Her eyes are just grey all over.'

Henrietta stared at her, intrigued. 'Hasn't anyone else noticed that? The other servants?'

'Marten hardly ever goes to the kitchens, or the servants' hall. She eats in her room, which is joined to Mama's. And you saw her just now, she wears that veil around her head. The others servants say it's because she's Talish, and it's a fashion, but I don't think that's it. It's so you'd have to look closely to see her eyes at all.' She lifted Henrietta onto her lap, and stroked her, over and over, calming herself as her fingers ran down the strange, smoothly rough fur. 'I try not to think about her, mostly. Do you think she's under a spell?'

Henrietta shivered. 'No. I think she *is* a spell.'

'She's made of magic?' Lily whispered, amazed. 'I didn't know you could do that.'

'Most people can't. It's not the sort of magic that any common-or-garden magician could manage. Arabel's father was a very learned sort of magician – he didn't do spells very often, although he could, when he wanted. Mostly he wrote about spells. And talked! On and on… Especially at lunchtime. But it was useful, sometimes. I remember him talking about spell creatures. Very, very difficult magic. And dangerous. I hadn't realised quite how strong your mother must be.' Henrietta looked suddenly mournful. It was an expression that suited her wrinkles. 'I was unkind to your sister. She is right to be so scared.'

'Really? She isn't just being feeble then?' Lily asked, in a small voice.

But Henrietta was suddenly pressing back against the window glass, her lips raising over her white teeth in a silent growl. Someone was coming out.

Lily strained her eyes, as if she could see through the dusty velvet if she tried hard enough. Even then, hiding behind a curtain from a spell-creature, her heart gave a sudden little bounce of excitement. Maybe she could? Every so often she would remember the magic that had brought her Henrietta and turn dizzy with happiness. It was mixed with a kind of delicious terror, but Lily knew she never wanted to give it up.

Lily could hear footsteps, and her mother's low,

musical voice. Then the footsteps pattered towards the door again, it opened, and Mama sailed through, with Marten following her close behind.

Lily dug her fingers into the crumbling wood of the window frame, to stop herself toppling out onto the floor in front of her mother. It was as though she was a magnet, and Lily a thin little pin, dragged towards her by a pull of painful spells. She wrapped the other arm around Henrietta, as the little dog's claws were squeaking along the painted wood, her eyes bulging at Lily in horror.

Only the merest hint of a paw slid out from behind the dark velvet, but it was enough that Marten's veiled head snapped round as she passed. Lily could feel the stony eyes scanning the window, and pressed herself even further into the corner, so close she was sure she could feel the grain of the wood imprinting her skin. Perhaps Marten would think it was only a mouse, she prayed, as the pull of Mama's magic died away.

There was a second's pause in the tapping footsteps over the stone, a faint hissing sound – and then they carried on, and Lily breathed.

The door creaking open again made them both jump, and Georgie's face appeared round it, looking anxious. 'Are you there, Lily?'

Lily unfolded herself creakily from behind the

curtain, and stepped out, Henrietta in her arms.

The pug was licking her paws frantically, as though she felt they might have been contaminated with something. 'She is horrible!' she hissed. 'I do not understand how the two of you could have such an unpleasant mother!' She glared suspiciously at Georgie. 'Or how you've managed to remain so comparatively – clean.'

Lily slipped into the library, and shut the door behind them, leaning against it and trying to catch her breath. Her heart was racing, and the air in the library seemed thick and dusty, so her breath came in unsteady gulps.

'It's the magic,' Georgie told her. 'It's even in the air in here. Breathe through your mouth – it helps, till you get used to it.'

Henrietta had wriggled down, and was trotting about the library, sniffing busily. When Merrythought had been a grand house, a place where magicians from all over the country, the world even, had gathered, the library had been their meeting place. It was the largest room in the house, even larger than the grand hall, and it ran through all the way to the back of the house, at almost double height, with a stained glass dome in the ceiling, surrounded by a little gallery. Lily had hardly ever been in it. She always wondered how the room managed to be so dark, despite all that glass, and the huge windows that looked out onto the old rose garden – which was a dandelion garden more than anything these days. But now she could see the magic swirling in the air, like dust motes in the sun, hazing everything.

'Georgie, did you know that Marten wasn't real? Henrietta says she's made of magic!'

Georgie shook her head. 'I don't think that's possible.'

'It is, and she is,' a little growly voice called back from inside one of the little bays of books that went around the walls. 'Although I suppose it might not have been your mother who created her.' She popped her head back around the shelves. 'She smelled of your mother's magic though, I think. Musky.'

'Why couldn't Mama just have a normal lady's maid?' Georgie sat down, as though her legs had given way under her. 'I can't even imagine the spells you'd need to do that! Where would you even start?'

Lily perched on the table next to her. 'With a body? Perhaps the spell's in one of these books.' They were everywhere – piled on the tables, spilling out of the shelves, even on the windowsills. The room stank of magic, and mouldy paper.

'A body!' Georgie stared at her in horror. 'Mama wouldn't! Would she?'

Lily swallowed. 'I only meant that I would start by trying to *make* the body… Did you think…? You really thought Mama might have stolen one from somewhere?'

Georgie shook her head. 'No. You thought it. I'm sure she wouldn't. I never said that!'

'It wouldn't surprise me in the slightest.' Henrietta had jumped from a large magical lexicon which had been abandoned on the floor, onto the chair next to Georgie's. Now she sat neatly curled on the embroidered cushion, watching Lily and Georgie with her head turned sideways. She seemed to think they were rather amusing. 'It might not have started as a human body, of course. Not that Marten's even human now.'

'Did Great Aunt Arabel do that sort of thing?' Georgie asked, fascinated.

'Certainly not! Only the very worst kind of magician would.' She turned her head over to the other side, slowly. 'You do realise this, don't you? That your mother is terribly dangerous.'

Lily frowned. She was frightened of her mother – she always had been, as far as she could remember, but she was rather proud of her at the same time. Things she had always known and understood seemed to be disappearing away from her all of a sudden. It was like standing on the sandy part of the beach, and feeling the sea rush in and steal the sand from between your toes.

'Is she really bad?' she whispered miserably, hoping that Henrietta might laugh, and say, *Of course not, only a little.*

Henrietta said nothing for a moment, pawing at her nose nervously. Then she sighed. 'I only knew Arabel until she was just a little older than you, Georgiana, but your family then were very different. They were strong magicians, but even so, they kept away from the darker spells, although Arabel's father loved to talk about them. Arabel and her sisters were taught the subtler sorts of magic. Glamours. Illusions. Twisting the weather. I'm not surprised she became a weather worker. Her spells always went wrong, but she had a talent for it, even then. The kind of thing your mother is doing is much more dubious. And half the books in this room should be under lock and key.'

Georgie was frowning. 'You don't know Mama. I don't see how you can say that sort of thing.'

Lily was so surprised she laughed, startled into agreeing with Henrietta after all. Of course the little dog was right. 'Georgie, she's had you under a spell so deep you practically forgot who I was! How can there possibly be a good reason for that?'

'Your sister has been with your mother a great deal

more than you have,' Henrietta said slowly, leaning closer to Georgie, and sniffing her suspiciously. 'It would be odd if she hadn't imbibed rather more of her magic – and her morals – than you. And she's probably still wrapped in the rags of that spell, too.'

'Stop sniffing me!' Georgie snapped.

'Was it cast in here, I wonder?' Henrietta turned her head to the other side again – it seemed to be what she did when she was particularly deep in thought. 'That would explain why she's slipping away again.'

'I'm not!' Georgie's eyes were blazing now. 'Really, you are the rudest creature I've ever met! And Mama has shown me several elemental creatures who were quite disgusting, I promise you!' She swallowed. 'I know Mama is planning something, and it's bad. But it's all I've ever been meant to do, Lily. It's like a rug being pulled out from under my feet – everything I know has changed, in less than a day.' She wrapped her arms around herself, and shivered. 'And you're right,' she admitted grudgingly to Henrietta. 'It *is* harder in here. The spell's still in the air, I'm sure, and it makes me want to do as I'm told.'

'Then we need to hurry and find – whatever it is we're looking for.' Lily stood up, looking around helplessly.

They walked around the library for a few minutes,

Lily taking out a book here and there, and glancing through it. At last she sank down in a corner of one of the bays with a hopeless sigh. 'This was a stupid idea! I thought it would be easier to find – as if they were going to leave a big piece of paper pinned up with *My Evil Plan* written across the top. There must be a thousand books in here, at least, and any of them might hold the spells that she wants you to do.'

'I don't think we ought to be looking for a book.' Georgie was standing at the desk that was drawn up to the window. 'This is where Mama sits to write. Shouldn't we be looking for something she's written down?' Then she turned back to Lily and made a face. 'I see what you mean. Something that says *My Evil Plan* on it. Oh, maybe it is stupid.'

'Not necessarily.' Henrietta had clambered onto one of the low shelves, and had been working her way around, sniffing curiously at the books, and sneezing disgustedly whenever she came to a particularly pungent one. 'After all, why would she need to hide her plans? She still thinks you are under a spell, Georgiana, and it seems to me, Lily, that she's entirely forgotten that you exist.' She had reached Lily's corner now, and she licked the tip of her ear sympathetically. 'Which is a very good thing. Anyway, if she has written anything, she might well have left it lying around.'

'Does she sit anywhere else?' Lily asked.

Georgie glanced around. 'Sometimes she sits in that armchair, over there. Or else she prowls about and creeps up behind me to tell me I'm doing something wrong.'

The armchair was drawn up close to the library fire, and books and papers were scattered all around it. It was upholstered in some dark, slightly shining fabric that reminded Lily of one of Mama's dresses. It smelled of her too, that strange musky smell that Henrietta had noticed in the magic around Marten. It was like one of the hot spices that Mrs Porter kept in earthenware jars on the dresser. No one was allowed to touch them, as they came from the East, and were expensive. Lily crept up on it sideways, and then felt foolish for being frightened of a chair.

Georgie was sorting through the papers on the desk, trying not to disarrange them too much and make it obvious they had been snooping.

'These are all about the old magical families...' she murmured. 'And a spell for planting seeds inside people – ugh, why on earth would Mama want to do that?'

Lily tiptoed around the armchair to look at the collection of odd things on a little piecrust table that stood next to the chair. A decanter of some strange dark cordial – which she had no desire to taste – a broken ivory and silver comb, and a book, covered in dull emerald leather. It was a fat little book, with worn golden lettering on the front. Lily had to frown to make it out, and at last she picked it up to see it properly.

Photographic Album, it read, in flowing, decorative letters.

A little card slipped out, painted with brownish, faded flowers, and a message in spidery writing. *For my dear niece Nerissa, on the occasion of your wedding day.* Nerissa was her mama's name.

Lily opened it gently, turning the brittle pages. The first photograph was a wedding portrait, with Mama seated on a spindly little chair, and Father behind her, looking rather grim. Lily stroked one finger gently over him – Mama had a painting of him, in a locket on her dressing table, but Lily had never seen it. Swallowing a little, she realised that if this man hadn't been pictured with Mama, she might have thought he was a stranger.

Frowning at the photograph, Lily decided that the odd-shaped bit of column they had been posed in front of was actually part of the gazebo at the centre of the sea of dandelions outside the library windows. Merrythought had still been rich and smart-looking then, even though the Decree had already come into force. The date written underneath was June, 1865 – twenty-five years ago.

'What is it?' Georgie asked, coming to look over her shoulder.

'Portraits – look, their wedding.' She turned the page. 'And Mama with a baby. Oh! This is Lucy. And she was born only a year after they were married – she would be twenty-four now, if she hadn't died…'

Henrietta leaped up onto the armchair to see the pictures too. 'How very interesting. Arabel and her sisters went to an exhibition of daguerrotypes in London once, and took me, but I have never seen anything like these. They all look rather miserable,' she added, wrinkling her nose as Lily turned the pages on several pictures of girls around her own age.

'You have to stand very still,' Georgie explained. 'That's why everyone always seems grumpy. It takes ages.'

'Lucy and Prudence,' Lily muttered, turning the pages. 'They were older than me, I think. They weren't babies when they died, Georgie. More your age, at least.' She bit her lip, glancing up at Georgie worriedly.

'Children die sometimes too.' Georgie's voice was stubborn. Then she sighed. 'But not two of them, surely? Unless they had typhoid, perhaps? But it would be terribly unlucky, to take both girls.'

'It didn't happen all at once, anyway. Lucy's gone in this one, see – it's only Prudence, and that must be you she's holding, Georgie,' Lily murmured.

'No photographs of any of them aged much older than you.' Henrietta nosed one of the pages to turn to the next portrait – Prudence, her light hair in long, soft ringlets. She looked as though she had been very well-named, her face sweet and biddable-looking. In fact, she looked remarkably like Georgie. Even down to the worried, frightened look in her eyes. She was holding the baby this time, a pretty fair-haired little lump. Prudence seemed to be eyeing her rather anxiously, but Lily wasn't sure if that was her imagination.

'She knows,' Henrietta muttered, and Lily shivered. Not her imagination then.

'The rest of it is empty,' she said, flicking through the fraying pages. 'Oh, except there's a pocket at the back.' She unfolded the little envelope, and drew out a piece of paper, which seemed much newer than the rest of the album. It was written in the darkest blue ink, in her mother's tight, spiky writing. 'It's a list of spells, I think,' she said doubtfully, handing it to Georgie.

'Yes.' Georgie frowned. 'All horrible ones. Just reading the names of them makes me shiver.'

'Show me,' Henrietta asked, scrambling up into Lily's arms and leaning over. 'Ugh. Not just horrible. I've heard of some of these. They're for killing people.'

Georgie shook her head. 'No. No, some of them are

dangerous, but they can't be for that. This one definitely isn't, look. I know this one. I've done it. I think.' She pointed to one of the lines halfway down the list.

Lily stared at her sister, wide-eyed, and Henrietta froze in her arms. 'Look at what it says underneath,' she growled softly.

Georgie glanced at them both crossly, and read out, 'Steals the breath and thins the blood. Eventually effective but rather slow.'

'Who did you cast it on?' Lily whispered, the words sticking in her throat.

'I – I don't know. Mama just told me to practise it, and I still can't remember properly…' Georgie dropped the piece of paper, and seemed to sway on her feet, clutching at the back of the chair to hold herself up. 'Have I killed somebody?'

Henrietta stared at her for a moment. 'I should think that depends on how well you did the spell.'

Georgie swallowed. 'She was very cross about it. She said I was useless. Oh, then perhaps I didn't! I can't have done… Can I?'

'Have you learned any more of them?' Lily asked, handing her back the piece of paper.

'Yes… This one. And this. About half the list, I think. But only to study. They're all such difficult ones. They need a lot of magic, and training, and even then it's a knack, I think. I haven't cast any of the others, I'm not even ready to try.' For the first time, Georgie looked relieved that she wasn't as good at magic as everyone wanted. 'Lily, Mama is teaching me to kill people,' she said flatly. And then she collapsed into the armchair, looking sick. 'I don't want to kill people… Who would?' She huddled back into the chair, small and lost against the cushions.

'Your mother, clearly,' Henrietta muttered, sniffing at the list, and sneezing as though it were peppery. 'Ugh…'

'I think it's one person.' Lily pointed to another spell. 'Look what she's written underneath this one. *Too hard to reach her*. These are all designed for one person in particular.'

Georgie frowned, and sat up. 'Is this how they did away with Lucy and Prudence and the others? Mama's trying to get me to learn spells to get rid of myself? That doesn't make sense.'

Lily shook her head. 'No. Think about it. *Her*. The one person Mama can't stand. The one who destroyed everything for us.'

Henrietta gave a sharp, excited little yap. 'Ah! I understand now. The queen, yes?'

Lily nodded, staring into her sister's troubled eyes. 'She's training you to assassinate Queen Sophia.'

FIVE

The two girls and the dog sat curled up together in front of the dying library fire, staring into the greying coals, and trying to make sense of what they had seen.

'That's what it's all about?' Georgie muttered. 'Getting rid of the queen?'

'It fits.' Lily nodded. 'It fits with the stories Mama was always telling you, the ones you passed on to me. That Queen Sophia is a terrible tyrant, and we have to put the magicians back in power again. The easiest way to bring the magic back would be to kill her, wouldn't it? She's the one forbidding magic, because she was so upset about her father's death.'

'I suppose so.' Georgie shrugged wearily. 'Perhaps it

isn't such a bad thing. She did have Father put in prison, you know.'

'Maybe he deserved it,' Lily said in a small voice, 'if he was plotting to assassinate the queen too. The Queen's Men just got in first…'

Georgie shook her head. 'No. That would be treason. I don't think they put you in prison for treason, Lily, they just hang you. He might have been in on Mama's plot, but he can't have been discovered. They would never have left Mama free either, would they? Or us. They would have put us all in prison. Regicides. That's what they call people who kill kings and queens.'

Lily nodded, and found herself holding Georgie's hand. Before Mama had started giving Georgie quite so many lessons, Lily's favourite thing of all had been to play with her sister. It was hard to remember, now that Georgie was so quiet and listless, but she had invented the most amazing games. Make-believe games. And their favourite had always been the same. They didn't play it often – partly so as not to spoil it, but mostly because they'd known it would be very unfortunate to be caught. They would find a cupboard – the linen cupboard in the old housekeeper's room was particularly good – and take turns to shut each other inside, or almost.

Actually, Lily refused to let Georgie shut the door completely as she was afraid of the dark, and Georgie refused to let Lily shut it because she didn't trust her not to wander off and forget about her. They would borrow a cup of water, and a crust of bread from Martha in the kitchen, and whoever was being the cruel jailer would take great delight in describing the enormous rats she had seen recently or the lingering death of the prisoner in the next cell.

It was only such a good game because of the terrifying feeling that one day it might come true. If the Queen's Men came unexpectedly, perhaps, and found that Mama had not renounced magic as she promised. If one of the servants talked... It could happen. Like it had happened to Father.

'Do you think he knew what Mama was doing?' Lily asked. 'He's only been in prison for nearly nine years. If we're right about Lucy, and Prudence, then Mama's been planning this for ages. A lot longer than that. Was he part of the plot too?'

Georgie pleated the edge of the piece of paper, and shook her head. 'I don't think so. I hardly remember him – I was only three, after all – but I don't think he would have done anything that might have hurt us.' She frowned. 'He was so *worried*, all the time. But I suppose if he had two little girls before us, two little girls who died, then that makes sense.' She smiled. 'He used to feed me cod liver oil.'

'Uurgh!' Lily shivered. Mrs Porter had a large brown glass jar of that, and she occasionally made Lily take spoonfuls. It was horrible.

'No, it was lovely. I think he'd changed the flavour, it tasted of roses. He gave it to you, too. Don't you remember? Pink stuff?'

Lily shook her head, staring at Georgie doubtfully.

'Well, he did. And he used to fuss if I so much as coughed.' Georgie frowned. 'It all makes sense now.'

'So Lucy and Prudence sickened for something,' Lily said quietly.

Georgie stared doubtfully at the list of spells again. She seemed unable to tear her eyes away from it – particularly the one she might have cast. 'You know, if Mama had ever let the Queen's Men see that we had any magic, we would have been taken away. There are awful places. Schools where they send magicians' children to have the magic stopped somehow. Perhaps she *ought* to be assassinated. Maybe Mama's doing the right thing. Sometimes people have to use desperate measures...' But she was biting her hair again.

Lily simply looked at her. And then she picked up the photograph album again, and held it out to Georgie, turning over the pages to show her their sisters.

Georgie nodded.

'We have to get away. Even if we did agree with

assassinating people – and I don't! – Mama's going to give up on you. We heard her say so. She's going to do the same thing to you that she did to the others! She probably will use one of the spells on that list, Georgie. She's given up on trying to teach you them, so she'll use one to get rid of you instead. Something that makes it look like you're ill. The blood-thinning one. We have to run away.' Lily stared at her sister, almost angrily, and then shook her. 'Georgie!'

'I know! But where will we go? Neither of us has ever left Merrythought, Lily. I don't know how to be anywhere else.'

'But I do.'

The two sisters turned to look at the little black dog sitting smugly between them.

'Merrythought is all very well for a country home, but I always found it rather too quiet.' Henrietta yawned. 'I much prefer London. Let's go there. Your mama would never find you in an enormous city, would she? And if your father is not involved in this plot, we had better find him, and tell him what his wife is doing.' She smiled wolfishly. 'After all, if she is discovered, he will not last long, will he? No one will believe he's innocent. Those evil magicians, even plotting in prison!' She gave a determined little nod. 'I think we should go soon – before she starts to turn her attention to you, Lily.'

Lily stared at her. Henrietta had only said what she had been thinking – she had even hoped that they might go to London – but someone else saying it out loud made it sound far more frightening. 'How would we get off the island? We'd need a boat. There is one, a rowing boat, in that little boathouse at the bottom of the cliff path, but it's always locked. Mr Francis has the keys in his pantry.'

Georgie frowned. 'I've seen letters from Father – not to read. Only the envelopes, and glimpses as she was reading them. I always searched for the letters afterwards, but Mama hid them, I think. They had London postmarks.'

Lily started suddenly, as a hand tapped her shoulder. She swung round, nearly tipping herself into the fire, and the small, dirty hand grabbed her sleeve.

Peter had lost his pale, starved look after three years of all the kitchen scraps he could steal, but he was still thin, and he still didn't talk.

'Were you listening?' Lily snapped.

'Lily! He can't hear!' Georgie whispered to her.

'He may not be able to hear, but he can still listen,' Lily told her, staring straight at Peter, and speaking very clearly so he could read her lips.

Peter grinned at her, and wriggled his hand to suggest he'd heard a little. Some. Enough.

'How did you creep up on us?' Lily demanded crossly.

Peter put down the box of firewood he'd brought in, and scrabbled in the pocket of his battered shirt, bringing out a piece of paper and a stub of pencil. He scrawled something on the paper, and handed it to Lily, smirking.

If you're running off, you need to get a lot better at it. Watch your backs.

'We didn't know you were sneaking around,' Lily muttered.

Henrietta had prowled all around him, sniffing at his feet. 'Could you steal the key to this boathouse?' she asked suddenly, scratching at his knee to make him look down at her.

Peter's eyes widened, so that they were almost as round as Henrietta's. All the servants knew that magic was going on in the house, but they hardly ever saw it. The girls' mother was careful, and Lily knew he had never seen anything like Henrietta. At last he nodded, and shrugged.

'You'd do that?' Lily frowned at him. 'Why don't you come with us?' she added hopefully, after a moment. 'We have to get away – Mama's had Georgie under a spell, and we think she might... She might do something very bad...' She couldn't bring herself to say that they suspected Mama was planning to get rid of Georgie, like so much rubbish. 'We're going to London!' she said instead. 'Please, Peter, come with us. Won't you?'

Peter stared at her, his eyes twitching from side to side as though someone were chasing him, but after a moment he shook his head regretfully.

'Not everyone on the mainland would be so bad.' Lily couldn't say *like the family who sent you here*, but they both knew that was what she meant.

I'll slide the key under your door, Peter wrote. Then he looked up at her, and added, *Tonight?*

Lily glanced at Georgie and Henrietta. The pug was nodding enthusiastically. Georgie swallowed, clenching her nails into her palms, and whispered, 'Yes.'

Lily nodded. 'Tonight.'

'Are you sure she keeps it in here?' Lily whispered, glancing over her shoulder in a hunted sort of way. It was past ten and the evening was darker now. They had only a candle, and the light was flickering on the furniture, sending shadows leaping here and there like ghosts.

Henrietta nodded, and put her front paws up against the dressing table chair. 'I can smell it. Gold has a very distinctive smell, Lily. Like butter.'

'Oh, do hurry! What if Mrs Porter's burned the dinner again? Mama might storm up here and be back any second,' Georgie moaned. She was lurking by Mama's bedroom door, supposedly keeping a watch on the passageway. They had taken a thin film of face powder from the pink china pot on the dressing table, and laid it over the threadbare carpet at the top of the stairs. If Georgie's spell had worked – which she said she was quite sure it hadn't, although Lily and Henrietta had chosen to ignore this as just Georgie panicking – then if anyone walked through the powder, the lid of the pot should clatter up and down. It was a very clever spell. If it worked.

'Georgie, how do we undo a lock spell? Mama's locked this drawer.'

'Ohhh…' Georgie ran back over to the dressing table, eyeing the powder pot miserably. 'It isn't a spell – it's really locked. Oh, honestly, Lily! The key's there, by the side of the mirror.'

'Oh.' Lily looked at the key rather disappointedly. She had been hoping for something a little more interesting. Swiftly she unlocked the drawer, and pulled out a small, red velvet bag, which was heavy, and chinked pleasingly in her hand.

'What's that under it?' Georgie asked, curious now, in spite of herself.

'Letters! Georgie, the letters from Father, they must be!' Lily drew one out with shaking fingers, and unfolded it. '*Dearest* – that must be from Father. *I have not had news from you in so long. Please write to tell me how my little daughters are faring. Are they still well and strong?* That's us, Georgie.' Lily blinked, her eyes suddenly stinging with tears. Hardly anyone worried about how she was, only Martha, and she was usually too busy running around after the cook to give Lily much thought. 'I suppose he hasn't much else to do in prison, except worry about us all,' she murmured sadly. '*I have been questioned again about this ridiculous plot. I protest my innocence, but they seem convinced. They must have some sort of evidence, but of course, they won't tell me what it is, so I cannot defend myself. I begin to think that I will never persuade them that I only wish to fight with words. I cannot agree with the law of the land – and if it were not for the damnable restrictions they place upon us, I would not be able to hold back my magic. How could I imprison it, if they were not imprisoning me? Perhaps they are right to keep me here, after all. But I would never stoop to plot against the queen.*' Lily looked up, her eyes shining with relief. 'He isn't part of it! There's no reason he should lie in a letter to Mama, is there?'

Georgie shook her head slowly. 'I suppose not. Unless he was trying to throw his guards off the scent.

But it doesn't sound like that.'

'Something's coming!' Henrietta suddenly hissed.

'Mama?' Lily looked down at the powder pot, and then whirled round to stare at Georgie and the door.

'No. Some*thing*. It's that spell-creature, and it isn't coming from downstairs. It was here all the time.' Henrietta was backing up against the bed, her nose tracking from side to side. 'Where is it?'

'She's in the anteroom. She's probably been listening,' Lily whispered, reaching down and scooping Henrietta up. 'I didn't even think about her. Peter's right, we're dreadful conspirators. We can't wait until midnight, Georgie, we'll have to go now. Marten will tell Mama everything.'

The door was opening already, and Lily watched, sickened, as a black-gloved hand slid around the side. She had never seen any of Marten's skin, she realised, swallowing. Perhaps she didn't have any.

'Run, run,' Henrietta growled. 'We don't know what she can do. Does she chase? Can she track us?'

'She doesn't need to, does she?' Lily gasped, as they flung themselves out of the bedroom door, leaving the door of the anteroom still slowly widening, and the darkness of Marten creeping around it. 'We were talking before we knew she was there. She must have heard us say we were running away, and the only way off the island is by the boat in the boat house.' They raced along the passage, not even noticing the face powder trap at the top of the stairs, until it puffed and shimmered around them. Far behind them in the bedroom, they could hear a faint clatter of china, as the pot shook out its alarm.

'It worked!' Georgie laughed half-hysterically as they ran down the stairs.

'Of course it did,' Lily muttered. 'Just because you can't do evil assassination spells, it doesn't mean you can't do everything else. And hopefully it will distract Marten for a moment or so. We'll use the orangery door, no one will be there, and it's the quickest way out to the cliff path, anyway. I hid the bags under the gorse bushes.'

'She's coming after us – or to the dining room,' Henrietta growled, watching over Lily's shoulder. 'I can smell her.'

'Hurry then.'

They raced along the passage to the orangery, flinging the glass doors open, and stumbled out through the night gardens. It was a moonlit night, but still the overgrown garden seemed full of confused and disturbing shapes, which only resolved themselves into familiar landmarks as they dashed past.

Lily risked a glance back at the house, its dark bulk

shining here and there with tiny lights. One of the lights was moving now across the dining room windows.

'She's gone to Mama. They'll be after us any minute,' she hissed to Georgie. 'Run faster!'

But Georgie had stopped dead with a sharp little gasp, as a bulky figure rose up in front of them.

Lily tried not to scream. How had Marten – or was it Mama already? – ended up in front of them?

But then the dark form came closer, and she realised it was too small for Mama or Marten, and the strange growths on either side of it were baggage – hers and Georgie's.

Peter stuffed Georgie's bag into her arms, made a strangled, urgent sort of noise, and jerked his head to tell them to hurry and follow him down a narrow little path through the gorse bushes.

'Is this the quickest way?' Georgie asked him, but of course he was in front of her, and it was dark, so he didn't answer. 'It looks like we're just walking into the bushes. Lily, this can't be right.'

'Shh. Peter knows where he's going. And I bet Mama doesn't know this path. It goes straight down to the cliff edge. I didn't know he meant to come and help us,' Lily gasped out, as they chased Peter through the gorse. The path was so narrow it looked as if had been worn there by the rabbits, and the spiky gorse seized at their hair and their dresses.

'There's a light coming out of the orangery door. Lily, come on!' Georgie seized Lily's hand and pulled her on faster. 'We can't be caught, we just can't. Mama will know we've been snooping. Who knows what they'll do to us both.'

'They can't risk losing both of you,' Henrietta pointed out. 'Whatever the plan is, clearly they need a child.'

'I'd rather be dead,' Lily muttered. She said it without properly thinking, but as they blundered on through the gorse in dismayed silence, she realised it was true. Lily could imagine nothing worse than to be bound in a spell the way Georgie had been. Days seemed to have flowed past her sister like water, marked only by those frightened moments when she'd dimly seen that something was wrong. But those strange glimpses had never lasted long, and as they swam away from her, she'd been left to struggle on, alone and forgetful.

At last they came out of the gorse thicket and onto the cliff path itself, its wide stone steps carved into the side of the island by the first Powers who'd built Merrythought. The boathouse sat at the bottom of the path, half built into the cliff itself, and protecting the family's boats from the wild seas.

The path petered out as they reached the jetty. Lily

put Henrietta down, fumbled in her dress pocket for the boathouse key, and unlocked the door with fingers that suddenly fumbled and slipped. At last she managed to haul it open, its creak echoing eerily in the black, watery space beyond the doors.

'I can't see…' Lily whispered worriedly. 'Where's the boat? We should have brought a lantern.'

'Oh!' Georgie sounded embarrassed. There was a moment of muttering, and then the boathouse was suddenly a place of ripples and shadows, as a soft silvery light glowed from Georgie's hands.

Peter made a frightened gasping noise, and Lily sighed admiringly. So useful, and so pretty. Perhaps Georgie could even teach her… Then she remembered they were running for their lives, and turned back to look for the little rowing boat she'd seen the butler use the one time she remembered him crossing to the mainland.

It floated almost at her feet, an oily puddle of water slopping disconcertingly around its boards as the sea rocked it up and down.

'There's water in it,' Henrietta pointed out gloomily. 'But it seems to be the best we have. Hurry. I can hear voices on the cliff top.'

Lily quickly undid the ropes that tied the boat to the metal rings on the jetty, and Henrietta jumped onto one of the wooden seats, skidding across it and digging in her claws with a whimper.

Peter threw Lily's bag in, and flapped his hands at Georgie – clearly he didn't dare touch her.

Georgie stepped into the boat, flinching as the water soaked into her stockings, and Lily climbed after her, leaving Peter to push them off. She caught his hand as he bent to shove them away. 'Won't you come? Please?'

But he only shook his head, and pointed upwards, making angry faces at her.

Lily's eyes filled with tears. She had not cried at the thought of leaving home, but Peter was the only friend she'd had, for so many years. 'You have to hide then. Don't let them see that you helped us!'

Peter nodded, and pushed the boat out towards the doorway while Lily fumbled for the oars. He groaned in panicked frustration as she tried to get them into the rowlocks, and then jumped into the water after them, stumbling along waist-deep to shove the boat further out into the true sea.

'Thank heavens it's calm,' Georgie whispered, staring fearfully at the rolling water ahead of them.

'Thank you!' Lily called softly back to Peter, as she dipped the oars into the water. 'I'll come back for you,' she added in a whisper. 'I hope…'

Her last sight of him was a wet bedraggled figure –

much like the smaller, thinner child she'd seen that first time three years before. He waved once, and then ducked quickly underneath the jetty, moulding himself against the pilings in the darkness.

'Do you know how to do that?' Georgie murmured in surprise, watching Lily struggling with the oars.

Lily shook her head. 'No,' she gasped. 'But we're moving, that's what matters. I don't mind where we end up, as long it's away from here. Can you see anyone? Are they on the path?'

'There's a lantern, I think. Stop glowing, Georgie,' Henrietta commanded. 'We don't want them to see us.'

Georgie looked down at her hands worriedly, and then leaned over the side and dipped them in the water. The light faded slowly away, leaving them out on the sea in black night. Suddenly the noise of the water seemed louder, slapping against the side of the boat, dripping and splashing as Lily tried to row.

'I can see lights in the other direction, too.' Henrietta had scrambled up to the little seat in the prow of the boat, and was staring ahead of them. 'That must be the village. Keep going, Lily! Faster!'

'I'm trying, but the oars don't seem to want to go where I want them to go.'

'Here, I'll take one.' Georgie wriggled forward, trying not to tip the boat, and sat next to her, taking the right-hand oar. Squashed together on the narrow wooden seat, Lily felt a sudden surge of happiness, one she almost felt she had no right to when they were running for their lives. But she had Georgie back, close enough to touch.

'Lily, watch out! You're about to drop that,' her sister hissed crossly. 'Listen, we have to do this together. Dip your oar in. Pull...pull...pull...'

'We're getting closer to the village,' Henrietta reported. '*Oof!*'

'What's the matter?' Lily didn't dare turn round to look at her. 'Henrietta, what happened?'

'The sea's getting rougher,' a small, rather spluttery voice told her. 'A wave came over the front and splashed me.' There was a scrabble of paws as Henrietta came back into the main part of the boat.

Lily stopped concentrating quite so hard on the rhythm of the oars, and looked around. Although it was still so dark, her eyes had adjusted a little, and she could see shapes, as though there were different shades of black. The waves were definitely higher.

'This isn't natural,' Henrietta said suddenly. 'It was almost a flat calm when we set out, and now this? This is a spell. Your mother has bewitched the sea.' Her voice had dropped to a half-whimper, and Lily realised with a jolt that the dog was scared. But seconds later Henrietta had wriggled past her, and was up on the bench seat in front of the girls, her paws on the coaming, barking defiantly at the water that slopped over her as the waves grew taller, and at the unseen magician on the beach.

Almost in answer, a wind began to shriek around the boat, whipping the waves up even higher, so that the boat plunged and spun around.

'Pull the oars in,' Lily cried. 'Henrietta, get down, you'll be swept overboard,' she called to the little black dog, who was still perched at the side in a frenzy of barking – but Henrietta was so angry she didn't seem to notice Lily's voice, or the water that swept past her, swallowing her angry barks.

Lily crawled forward against the wind to try to grab her, but Georgie caught her skirt. 'Lily, you have to get down, the waves will take you!'

'I have to get Henrietta!' Lily screamed in her sister's ear.

'Then I'm holding on to you!' Georgie yelled back. 'I'll hold the seat and you, while you grab her.' She seized Lily's ankle and gripped it tightly, all the while muttering the words of a spell that Lily didn't think was working.

Lily reached out and tried to catch Henrietta, but the little dog bounded away, skittering across the seat to the other side of the boat to bark furiously at the walls of water on the other side.

'Come back!' Lily wailed, tears filling her eyes once more. She lunged after Henrietta, but the boat tipped, and she found herself hanging half out into the water.

'Lily!' she heard Georgie scream after her, and she wriggled back a little, sobbing, and watched in the darkness as her silvery tears fell into the sea.

'That was clever,' an interested voice said from by her shoulder. 'Did you do it on purpose?'

Lily sat up, and caught the glint of Henrietta's huge black eyes in the darkness.

'It stopped,' she murmured.

Georgie was uncurling herself from the bottom of the boat. 'What did you do? I was trying, but I'm sure it wasn't me.'

'She cried,' Henrietta said smugly. 'When her tears hit the water, she broke your mother's spell. You're rather good at breaking spells, Lily.'

'The storm swept us closer to the mainland, look!' Georgie pointed ahead. The sea was thumping against a rock-strewn beach, and the current seemed to be pulling the little boat onto the shore. They sat huddled together, shivering in their soaking wet clothes, as the friendly waves swept them closer in. At last, there was a soft crunching sound, and the boat grounded on the sand.

Lily climbed over the side, hardly noticing the water splashing round her boots, and looked around them. The lights from the village up on the top of the cliff were going out now, and the darkness was so thick she could almost touch it. She heard a splash as Georgie climbed out of the boat too, and went wading up onto the beach. Lily leaned back over the boat. 'Shall I lift you?' she asked Henrietta. 'It's still up past my ankles.'

There was no answer.

'Henrietta, what is it? I won't let you get wet.' Lily laughed. 'I know you're soaked already, but it's different jumping into it.'

There was a scuffling noise, and Henrietta came closer, and nuzzled her hand. 'I don't know if I can.'

Lily ran a hand over her damp fur. 'Why?'

'I'm a family dog. Part of your family, your magic. I belong in the house, in that portrait. This is a Merrythought boat still. But once I step onto the land...'

Lily stopped stroking, and stared at the little lump of darker night that was Henrietta. She had known her for only a day and a half, and she couldn't imagine what she would do if the pug disappeared. 'What would happen to you?' she stammered. 'Will you just go back to the painting? Why didn't you say?'

'It wouldn't have made any difference.' Lily could feel Henrietta's shrug. 'You had to go. And you needed me to help you get away, even if all I did was make you cry at just the right moment.'

'You can't.' Lily put her arms round Henrietta tightly, making sure not to pull her away from the boat. 'You can't go back to that painting. I won't let you.'

'I might not. I simply don't know.' Henrietta sounded offhand, as though she was discussing whether or not to drink a cup of tea, but Lily could hear her voice shaking, just a little.

'Lily! Are you coming?' Georgie splashed back towards them. 'Shall we walk up to the village? It's awfully dark, I don't know what would be best... We don't want anyone to see us, but it would be easy to get lost...'

'I think we should spend the night here,' Lily murmured distractedly. She couldn't bear the thought of taking Henrietta out of the boat in the dark. She wanted to see her again, properly, at least once more.

'At dawn,' Henrietta whispered in her ear, and Lily nodded.

Lily woke, cramped and frozen, with Henrietta curled in a ball of black fur on her lap. Georgie was lying next to her, with her head resting on the sodden bag of clothes she'd brought with her. The boat was rocking gently as the tide came in, and the sky was a soft rose-pink, streaked with yellow as the sun came up. She gazed wearily over the side of the boat to the beach. Soft biscuit-brown sand spread up to grassy dunes, so unlike the grey rocky cliffs of Merrythought that it seemed another world. How could the two places exist, less than two miles from each other?

The world across the sea had come to seem almost imaginary, since Lily had dreamed of it for so long. Now that she was here, and it was so clearly real, Lily found herself wondering if she were the dream. A strange, half-grown magician's child, with no proper understanding of magic. She sounded unreal, even to herself.

'Shall we try?' Henrietta had woken, and was standing on her lap, digging in her sharp little claws as she fidgeted anxiously back and forth.

Lily nodded, wriggling out from under Georgie, and leaving her sister sleeping. Stretching out her cramped legs, she scrambled over the side of the boat, hissing at the cold of the water as it sloshed around her ankles. Then she held out her arms to Henrietta, and the little dog closed her eyes and leaped.

Lily hugged her tightly, standing there in the water, waiting for her arms to suddenly be empty. But it didn't happen. When she opened her eyes, Henrietta was still there, looking slightly surprised.

'Well. Good.' She shook her ears in relief. 'Perhaps it's because I'm with a Merrythought girl,' she told Lily, licking her cheek. 'Shall we go and explore?'

SIX

'Lily, look! We did it. We're here…' Georgie was sitting up, staring around her in amazement. She climbed out of the boat, and stepped onto the sand, holding her damp skirts out in front of her as if they were a party dress. 'It was too dark to see last night, and I was so tired. But now…' She went dancing off up the sand, twirling and laughing like a mad thing.

Lily and Henrietta exchanged surprised glances. Lily hadn't seen her sister like this in years – always she had been pale and worried-looking, scared that her spells weren't working, and terrified their mother would find out. Now it was as if Georgie was the little sister, dancing to some gleeful music only she could hear.

'We have to look after her…' Lily murmured to

Henrietta, following Georgie up the beach.

'Mm.' The little dog nodded. 'Someone needs to. Really. Look at her!'

Georgie wandered back to them smiling dazedly, her damp blonde hair frizzing out like the floss silk trim on some of Mama's dresses.

'We look a sight,' Lily said, suddenly glancing down at her damp, crumpled skirt, and salt-stained boots. 'We should change before we set off.'

Georgie shook her head, seeming to come back to her senses again. 'The bags got wet too, remember? All our clothes will be wet. I'll do my best to dry us out as we walk. I remember a spell I found in the library. There was a handwritten book, something that one of the great-great-aunts had made. It was full of spells for things like that. Polishing furniture, and getting rid of ants in the kitchen. Mama said it was all nonsense, but I liked it.'

Lily nodded, and swallowed. 'Should we go, then?' she asked quietly.

Georgie turned to look back at the boat, and then across the water to the greyish lump that was the island in the dawn light.

'I suppose we should.'

'Isn't it strange to be somewhere else,' Lily whispered to her, and Georgie nodded.

'I don't know how to be, away from there,' she murmured.

'What you have to be is careful,' Henrietta warned her. 'If all magic is really outlawed now, you mustn't let any slip. Make sure this clothes-drying spell doesn't glitter, or anything silly like that.'

'I'd forgotten,' Georgie said, her eyes widening. Then she smiled, and said slyly, 'You realise you're going to have to keep quiet, don't you?'

Henrietta looked horrified for a second, and then she glared at Georgie. 'Of course I do.' But Lily was almost certain she hadn't thought of it. She set off up the beach, wanting to distract Henrietta before she said something unforgivable to her sister, which she thought the pug was quite capable of doing. Probably she would enjoy it.

A footpath ran along the top of the beach, leading to the village, which was only just starting to stir. The girls could hear a woman singing to herself as she lit her fire, the smoke spiralling delicately from the little chimney of her cottage.

'We should get through the village quickly,' Lily murmured, shaking herself. She wanted to stop and stare. It was all so strange. 'They'll know where we've come from. It won't be long before Mama comes searching, it's better no one sees us.'

'Your mama might think you're both drowned,'

Henrietta said, out of the corner of her mouth, after a quick glance from side to side.

Lily shook her head. 'I think she'd have rescued us, wouldn't she? Or perhaps she thought Georgie would save us somehow. After all, she needs us – one of us.'

'Maybe she was too angry to think straight. Working the sea must have worn out her magic for a while.' Georgie shivered, hurrying on between the cottages. 'Which way is it to Lacefield?'

They were coming to a slightly wider track now, which met the footpath at right angles. 'There's a sign, look.' Lily hurried on, and they stood looking up at the signpost. 'Lacefield, three miles that way.'

Lily knew that all the supplies for the house came from the grocer's at Lacefield, and that whenever anyone had visited – although Lily wasn't sure she'd ever seen anyone apart from the family, and the yearly visits of the Queen's Men – they had come by train to the station there. Eventually the train would wind its way through the countryside to Paddington station. London. Where they could hide out while they searched for their father.

'Stay by the hedges,' Henrietta muttered. 'Then if we see anyone coming, we can crawl through and hide in the fields.'

'But what shall we do when we get to Lacefield?'

Georgie said worriedly. 'We won't be able to creep through a town without anyone seeing us. And at the station we'll have to buy tickets, and ask about the trains. Someone might recognise us as the children from Merrythought House.'

'Can you do a glamour yet?' Lily asked her hopefully. She had read about glamours. They were a particular sort of spell designed to make people see one quite differently. It was quite technical, and all to do with confusing the way people's eyes and minds connected things together.

'I *think* I could, but only if I had time to sit and concentrate. And I might need some sort of amulet to help.' Georgie sighed. 'I didn't pack anything like that. Mama would have noticed if I'd taken anything from the library. I only brought a few basic ingredients, and the books I had in my room. I waterproofed them,' she added proudly.

Lily was just about to say that it would have helped if Georgie had waterproofed *all* the baggage, when Henrietta suddenly gave a meaningful sort of squeak, and nipped her ankle. Lily looked around wildly and realised with horror that an old man was walking towards them, leading a horse and cart. It was far too late to hide now.

'Brazen it out,' she muttered to Georgie, who looked

as though she had been sentenced to death.

Georgie gulped, and nodded. She pasted a sickly sort of smile onto her face, stood up straighter, and nodded to the man as he and the horse plodded past.

Lily smiled too, but she was waiting for the man to stare, and demand to know where they had come from. They had been walking through deserted fields and patches of woodland – no more villages, or indeed any signs of life, apart from a few disinterested sheep. He was probably from the village by the beach, returning home after a trip to the market in Lacefield, perhaps. He would know that they weren't village girls. Despite the salt stains, and the damp, and Lily's dress being made for a girl at least two years younger than she was, they were clearly dressed as young ladies, even if they had sopping wet boots on. A village child probably wouldn't have had boots at all, sopping or otherwise.

But although the man glanced at them curiously, all he did was tip his hat out of politeness, and venture a gruff, 'Good morning, miss, and to you, miss.'

'Good morning,' Georgie told him, smiling more naturally, and Lily added, 'Good morning to you.'

And they carried on, trying to turn round to see if he were staring after them, or whether he was setting off at a run to call the constable, and accuse them of being dangerous runaways.

'He didn't even look back,' Henrietta whispered. She had been watching openly – after all, as far as he knew, she was only a dog.

Lily couldn't help feeling a little insulted, although she knew that it was silly. He might have been at least a little interested in who they were.

'I suppose we never, ever come off the island,' she said quietly.

'Thank goodness, or they might have recognised us,' Georgie agreed.

'I wonder who he thought we were, though,' Lily went on.

Henrietta sniffed. 'He was probably more worried about the price he got for his vegetables at the market than he was about two scruffy children.'

Lily opened her mouth to protest, and then shut it again as she looked at Georgie. Her sister was a sight, and she was sure that she looked just as bad. 'Maybe we don't need to worry about Lacefield and the station,' was all she said. 'Perhaps no one will care.'

'What they'll care about is the gold,' Henrietta snapped. 'And that it's in the hands of two little ragamuffins. You'll have to furbish yourselves up a bit, before you go flashing that purse around.'

'What about the not-talking?' Georgie said sweetly.

Henrietta gave a little low growl. 'There's no one to

see me. Stop talking yourself, and get on with using those housekeeping spells you were boasting about. Get the wrinkles out of your dress, and your sister's, and for heaven's sake, girl, do something about your hair. Though I suppose at least it's clean now, which it wasn't when I first met you.'

Georgie flushed pink with crossness, which Lily noticed with surprise made her look much prettier. 'I was under a spell!' Georgie hissed.

'Well, that's your excuse,' Henrietta retorted, her eyes snapping, and the curl of her tail looking very tight and warlike.

'Can I help with the spell?' Lily asked hopefully, wanting to distract Georgie and Henrietta from each other.

Georgie turned and scowled at her. 'No!' Then she huffed and turned her back pointedly on Henrietta. 'Oh, very well, I suppose so. We need something to straighten out. The grass stems will do, can you pick a handful?'

She pointed at the faded brownish grasses at the foot of the hedge, and Lily, uncertainly, plucked a few stems. She had no idea how this was going to have anything to do with her crumpled dress.

'Scrunch them up a bit in your hands,' Georgie commanded. 'I suppose there really isn't anyone coming, is there?' she added worriedly. 'Perhaps just for this bit we ought to hide over by those trees. I can't guarantee it won't shimmer.'

There was a little clump of trees further on, and they scuttled towards it, hurrying into the shadowy dimness, and sighing gratefully. It was still only very early, but the sun was beating down hard already.

'Here, spread them out on my lap,' Georgie explained, sitting down on a fallen tree. 'Then listen, and you say it too. I hope I can remember it properly.'

Henrietta sniffed, but she had jumped up onto the tree too, and was sitting next to Georgie and staring interestedly at the grasses.

Georgie began to tease the crumpled stems through her fingers, humming in a low tone which Lily hoped didn't mean she had forgotten the words. Then she began to chant, slowly and sweetly,

Threads weave and ribbons coil,

Silks press, linens boil,

Stitch and sponge, irons from the fire,

Clean and straighten my attire. You too, Lily!' she hissed, twitching the grass stems straight in her lap. She glared crossly as Henrietta leaned over and seized a piece of grass in her teeth, pulling it to lie neatly with the others. 'Say it again!'

Together they repeated the spell, until all the grasses were lying in smart rows.

'Very impressive. Stand up,' Henrietta said, sitting down on the fallen tree now, her collar gleaming. It even had little golden studs on the pink leather, which Lily was certain hadn't been there before. 'Oh, much better! Even your hair,' she added to Georgie, with her head thoughtfully on one side.

Lily agreed with her. Even though Georgie was scowling, her hair was hanging in pretty waves, and her yellow muslin frock was spotless, its frills sharp-edged, as if they'd been ironed by a lady's maid. Lily twisted, trying to see herself, and then gasped in sudden realisation. The unpleasant tightness round her middle – which she'd been used to for months – had gone. Her dress actually fitted her. 'You made it bigger!' she told Georgie admiringly.

'*We* did.' Georgie nodded. 'I'm sure my spells work better when you say them too, Lily. Look, even your boots are polished.'

Lily pointed one toe out in front of her, admiring the mirror-like gloss. They were quite as good as Mr Francis's Sunday uniform boots, and he had been in the Seventh Hussars, as he never failed to remind everyone in the servants' hall.

'We look as though we might be able to afford our railway fares, I think,' she said happily. 'The bags look smarter too, not so scuffed. Now we just have to keep ourselves clean all the way to the town.'

'I've driven this way with Arabel,' Henrietta said, nosing out between the trees. 'I recognise it now. It isn't far.' She trotted out onto the lane, and looked back at the girls impatiently. 'Well, come along!'

Lacefield was not a large town. But for two girls who had lived secluded on an island their whole lives, it seemed enormous, and frighteningly busy.

Lily slipped her hand into Georgie's and stared as a smart carriage rumbled by, drawn by two glossy chestnut horses. There was a coat of arms painted on the door panel – the carriage must belong to some grand family in a big house nearby. Horses were awfully large, she decided, stepping a little further back from the roadway. She hadn't expected them to be that big, somehow. But so shiny, and the way the harness jingled! She felt like laughing out loud from pure excitement, and she couldn't help skipping, just a little.

'We'll have to ask someone where the station is,' she murmured.

Henrietta gave a tiny nod. Now that there were people all around, she was obviously trying very hard to be discreet.

'We could ask him,' Georgie suggested, pointing to a bored-looking boy sweeping the street outside a greengrocer's shop, although he was more leaning on the broom than actually sweeping with it. He stared at them curiously as they came closer.

'Could you tell us where the station is, please?' Lily asked him, as politely as she could, but he only gaped at her.

'The railway station?' Georgie added helpfully, as the silence lengthened, and eventually he nodded, and pointed to the end of the street. 'Down there, and turn left,' he muttered.

'Have you noticed,' Georgie muttered worriedly as they followed his directions, 'that every other girl we've seen has a hat on? And gloves? Perhaps that's why he stared so.'

'He still is,' Lily reported, having turned round to check. 'But I shouldn't think much that's exciting happens to such a boring boy.'

'Don't wave at him!' Georgie told her, shocked. 'I'm quite certain that's unladylike.'

'Well, he went pink and he's pretending to sweep again now, so maybe,' Lily agreed. 'There's a lot to learn, isn't there? Do you think there's anything we can do about the hats? You couldn't whip up a couple out of dock leaves, or something?'

'Here? Are you mad?' Georgie hissed.

'No, I suppose not. Well, we'll just have to be strange

then.' But now Georgie had pointed it out, it did seem that everyone was eyeing them in surprise, and they started to walk faster. 'I don't think I'd mind as much if they were talking about us behind our backs because they suspected we were dangerous magicians. But it's stupid that they're fussing about hats.'

'Just come on. Look, I can see the station.' Georgie grabbed her hand and pulled her along, as Lily eavesdropped on two very smartly dressed ladies.

'Are they Mrs Enderby's granddaughters? I wouldn't be surprised. Really, the woman has no idea of proper behaviour.'

'I bet I'd like her,' Lily muttered as Georgie hurried past her and into the little station building, which was red brick with curly white ironwork.

'I suppose we just go and buy a ticket,' Georgie muttered, looking uncertain. 'I know I've read about tickets in the newspaper. There was a terrible scandal about how expensive they are.'

Henrietta trotted further into the station, and jerked her head at them meaningfully, clearly pointing out a window where a man in a peaked cap with a lot of silver braid, and a large handlebar moustache, was eyeing them rather distrustfully.

'We'd like to go to London, please,' Lily said firmly, marching up to the window, and searching in the pocket of her dress for the little bag of stolen gold.

'Indeed.' The man sniffed disbelievingly. 'Ten shillings. For first class.' He glared down at the girls, clearly expecting them to giggle and run away. He looked positively gobsmacked when Lily produced a gold sovereign from her pocket, and handed it to him.

'When is the next train, please?' Georgie beamed at him.

'In about an hour,' the man stammered, pulling on his moustache and staring at them as he handed Lily a pile of coins. 'Platform one.'

Lily resisted the urge to run as they made their way to the platforms. She had a dreadful feeling that the man was going to run after them, shouting that they must have stolen the money – which of course they had.

They collapsed, giggling, on a bench on the platform, and Henrietta barked sharply at Lily, demanding to be picked up. Then she snuggled against Lily's shoulder, so she could whisper unobtrusively in her ear.

'How much money do we have?'

'Twenty of those sovereigns,' Lily told her. 'It isn't a lot, is it? I hadn't thought much beyond getting away from the island. What shall we *do* in London? We'll need more money before long.'

'I think we should worry about getting there first.'

Georgie leaned close, so as to join their whispered conversation. 'Let's just get as far away from Mama and Merrythought as possible.'

Lily nodded. The mad excitement of their escape was fading, for both of them, and the station was growing busier. People were walking down the platforms, and the station staff all wore dark uniforms. Each time a porter appeared, Lily felt her heart shudder, convinced that Marten was after them in her gleaming black dress.

Georgie shot a nervous glance around the platform. 'All Mama had to do was create another boat somehow, you know. Or just send Marten. Who knows what that creature can do? Perhaps she can walk on water? If she's made of spells, she can do anything.' Georgie shivered. 'We shouldn't have stayed on the beach last night. What if she'd come hunting for us over the water? We should have kept going!'

'In the dark? And I shouldn't think there were trains in the night.' Lily hugged her sister. Henrietta was right – Georgie was fragile. Too fragile for an adventure like this one. She could feel her shaking. 'We would have been in just as much danger here.'

'I suppose...' Georgie pulled away from her quickly, glancing back at the station building. 'Shhh!'

A tall, thin woman in a startlingly bright green travelling dress was marshalling a group of children, two servants, and an enormous mountain of baggage, onto the platform. At least three of the children seemed to be determined to throw themselves onto the railway line, preferably taking with them a large red parrot in an ornate golden cage.

Henrietta stiffened on Lily's lap, bristling at the bird, which she seemed to regard as an insult. It took one look at her and agreed, letting off a series of ear-splitting shrieks, which ended with what sounded like, 'Foul mongrel!'

The three little boys went into fits of laughter, one of them even rolling along the ground, temptingly close to Lily's foot. She restrained herself, merely patting Henrietta, and murmuring, 'Horrible mangy thing!' just loud enough for the parrot to hear. It probably had no idea what it was saying, but still.

The woman in the bright-green dress, and the girl with her, stared down their remarkably long pale noses – they had to be mother and daughter – at Lily and Georgie, and then smirked at each other in a way that made Lily want to leap up and scream.

'What are they looking like that for?' she hissed to Georgie.

'Probably the hats again,' Georgie muttered. 'I mean look, hers would make at least three hats.' It was true that the mother's hat was loaded with so much lace and flowers and feathers, plus a veil, that it must have made her neck ache.

'Shh, I want to listen,' Lily hushed her. The girl was whispering, but in the loud, hissy sort of whisper that was clearly meant to be heard.

'I don't think either of them are wearing corsets! And they've obviously never even heard of a dress-improver!' she sniggered.

'What's a dress-improver?' Lily nudged Georgie. 'Is it whatever's making her bottom stick out like a beetle?'

'She'll hear you! Oh, Lily, look! The train!'

Puffing grandly towards them was what looked like a large black and golden dragon, belching out steam, and even sparks, so that it seemed to be surrounded by clouds of fiery smoke.

'But magic isn't supposed to be allowed!' Lily hissed to Georgie, her eyes wide with horror, almost expecting a detachment of Queen's Men to arrest them all on the spot.

'It isn't magic. It's all done with pistons – and – and things,' Georgie muttered, although she was half hiding behind Lily, and she had her hair in her mouth again.

'It *looks* magic,' Lily whispered, her eyes shining. 'I thought it was a dragon. Wouldn't a dragon be wonderful?'

'No,' someone muttered very quietly by her

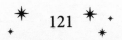

shoulder, and Lily scratched Henrietta's ears. She looked unnerved by the train too, her eyes bulging even more than usual.

'London train! All aboard!' It was the man from the ticket office, roaring and stomping up and down the platform with a flag. The smart family with the parrot were twittering around, trying to make sure they hadn't left anything behind, and Lily snatched up her bag, and hurried to one of the black-and-cream-painted carriages. Then she went back for Georgie, who was still sitting open-mouthed on the bench, and hustled her in, shooing her into a little box-like room inside the carriage, so she could collapse onto a velvet-covered seat.

'I never thought trains would be so big,' Georgie muttered, clutching the edge of the window and looking panicked as the huge machine shuddered and throbbed, and drew away.

Lily stood in the corridor with Henrietta in her arms, watching as the little station seemed to slip away from them. Henrietta was wheezing with excitement, her little curl of a tail shaking. 'So fast!' she muttered. And then she darted her head forward sharply. 'Look!'

Lily looked. Standing alone on the platform was a still black figure. The long black dress trailed the ground, covered in a black cloak. Now the black veil was swathed around a close-fitting black bonnet.

Marten.

They watched her as the train hurried away, the rhythm of the wheels stilling the racing of their hearts.

'She didn't catch the train,' Henrietta pointed out. 'We can be thankful for that.'

'But she knows where we're going,' Lily murmured, her cheek still pressed against the chill glass of the window. Then she straightened up, glancing back at Georgie in the compartment, who was sitting quite upright on the very edge of the seat, staring out of the other window, her teeth biting into her lip. 'We don't tell her!' she hissed to Henrietta.

The dog eyed Georgie thoughtfully, and nodded. 'No. Better not.' She wriggled down from Lily's arms, and trotted into the compartment, beckoning Lily to follow with a jerk of her head. Then she busily shoved the sliding door closed with her bottom, and turned back to the girls, her eyes sparkling. 'I do trust neither of you suffer from motion sickness?' she asked, as Lily lifted her onto the seat, and she sat staring around her regally.

'It can't be worse than the boat,' Lily pointed out. 'I do wish we'd brought sandwiches, actually. I should think London is quite a long way away, isn't it?'

SEVEN

'There's just so much of it...' Lily murmured, staring out of the carriage window as the landscape sped by. 'I know Merrythought was only a very small island, but I hadn't thought there'd be so much of everywhere else...'

Georgie nodded. 'All those houses – all those people!'

They had just wheezed out of another station, in a middling sort of town.

'London is a great deal bigger than that, you know,' Henrietta pointed out helpfully. She seemed to find their amazement rather funny.

Lily nodded. 'I suppose it must be.' She sank back against the padded train seat, letting the view out of the window become a greenish blur. 'What are we going to do when we get there?' she asked, in a small voice. 'I hadn't thought much further than getting away from Mama.'

'Well... We'll have to find somewhere to stay. A boarding house, I suppose,' Georgie said slowly. 'And then try to find out where Father has been imprisoned. His letters have a London postmark, but the envelopes have a different handwriting. The Queen's Men read them before they're sent to Mama, I suppose, and that means they might have sent them on to London first, and the prison isn't there at all. But it's somewhere to start.' She gave a rather hopeless sigh.

Lily nudged her. 'Georgie, don't be miserable! You can't – we must be about a hundred miles away from home!'

Georgie stared at her. 'I know! That's *why* I'm miserable!'

'But aren't you excited?' Lily asked her. 'How can you miss home, when you think about what Mama was planning?'

'I don't know, but I do.' Georgie sighed again. 'I don't like all this bigness.'

Henrietta sniffed, and eyed her thoughtfully. Lily saw her give Georgie the same slightly worried look nine hours later, when they stumbled out of the carriage –

into the madness of Paddington Station, at five o'clock in the evening.

'The whole of our house would fit in here,' Lily whispered, staring around at the cavernous building. It was still light outside, but round glass gas lamps were suspended from the delicate iron trellises in the arched roof, burning like a hundred little moons. There were even pigeons flying about under the glass.

'The newspaper said that all the trains into Wales and the West start from Paddington,' Georgie murmured, her eyes so wide that the whites showed all round. 'I suppose it would be big. But still…'

They stood huddled next to their train, ignored as the crowd boiled and hustled around them. Across the platform another train stood steaming, ready to set off, while passengers swirled around the doors, fussing at the stowing of their baggage, and porters raced up with trolleys piled with yet more bags.

'Lily, there's a pig in that crate,' Georgie pointed out in amazement, staring at a slatted wooden crate that had been abandoned close to them.

'Poor thing,' Lily murmured, bending to peep through the cracks. The pig looked distinctly confused and annoyed, and squealed at her indignantly. Rather a lot of the passengers turned round to see what was happening and Lily tried hard to look as though it were nothing to do with her.

'Come on,' Georgie picked up both bags. 'You had better carry Henrietta, someone might step on her in here.'

'They might regret it,' Lily giggled, and Henrietta licked her lovingly.

They hurried through the bustling station, dodging porters, and newspaper sellers, and people running after their trains, making for the grand arch out onto the street.

'Gracious,' Henrietta whispered. 'What a lot of omnibuses. Ah! Look! That one is for Bloomsbury, it's painted on the side. Lots of boarding houses there, or there always used to be. Hop onto it, quickly, before it goes!'

Two enormous horses, one black, one grey, were pulling a heavy, wheeled carriage, painted black and red, its roof piled high with parcels and people, with an elderly gentleman in a frock coat just climbing inside. Lily and Georgie ran a little way down the road, and clambered in after him.

'Where to, miss?' demanded a man in a battered top hat, brandishing a jingling satchel.

'Bloomsbury,' Lily said promptly, even though she had no idea where that was. Henrietta panted at her approvingly.

'Penny each. And make sure the dog's under control, miss, we don't properly allow dogs, but I'll make an exception, see?'

Lily nodded, and ferreted in her purse, trying not to show the gold coins.

'Look at it,' Georgie murmured, staring out of the grubby window. 'We thought Lacefield was busy.'

'It's like the ants' nest I found in the gazebo,' Lily agreed, staring at the churning mass of carriages and the people hurrying through the streets. 'And all those shops!'

The omnibus was rattling along the side of an enormous park, which seemed to have a river running through it, but soon it was back into busy streets again, the driver shouting angrily as carriages swerved around him, and once a little boy and a dog raced across the road.

'How are we ever going to live here?' Georgie turned away from the window, looking anxiously at Lily. 'There were twelve people at Merrythought, Lily, only us and the servants. There must be thousands – *millions* – of people in this city.'

'I know. Isn't it wonderful?' Lily sighed happily, and then caught Georgie's look of horrified amazement. 'Georgie, millions of people, and only two of us!'

Henrietta nipped her wrist meaningfully.

'*Three*, ow. They'll never find us, Georgie, never!'

'I suppose you're right,' Georgie murmured, turning back to look out of the window again, and eyeing the crowd around a butcher's shop. 'As long as we don't draw attention to ourselves.' She looked at Henrietta as she said it, and the pug glared back at her in outrage.

'Bloomsbury!' the man in the top hat yelled, and the girls stumbled through the grubby straw around their feet to the door of the omnibus, thanked him politely, and watched it rumble away.

Bloomsbury, they realised as they stepped out into the growing dusk, was a much quieter area of the city. Tall grey houses lined the streets, and only the occasional carriage rattled past.

'Look in the windows,' Henrietta hissed up at Lily. 'Lodgings! That's why I brought us here!'

'Oh!' Lily turned to look at the house they were standing by, and saw that it did indeed have a card in the corner of the window. *Lodgings available. Respectable persons only need apply.*

'Do lodging houses have food?' she said hopefully. 'It's almost a whole day since we've eaten anything…'

'I know!' Henrietta hissed.

Georgie glared at her. 'Shhh, you! Lily, do you think we are respectable?' she asked anxiously. 'Without hats on? That old gentleman in the omnibus was muttering about it, I could hear him.'

'Couldn't we just be eccentric?' Lily suggested. 'Let's try.' She ran up the steps, and tugged the bell pull sharply. She could hear it jangling away inside the house, but no one came, so she pulled it again, even harder. This time the bell seemed to be fairly dancing inside, and there was a patter of swift, angry footsteps.

The woman who opened the door was stout and dark-haired, rather like Mama, except that she was wearing a blouse with the most enormous leg-of-mutton sleeves – as though someone had blown them up like a balloon, and a huge apron all round her middle. Mama had probably never worn an apron in her life.

Lily smiled, and was just about to inquire about the lodgings, when the woman stuck her hands on her hips and demanded, 'Whatever do you mean by pulling on the bell like that? It's a mercy it isn't broken! What on earth do you want?'

'Rooms…' Lily stammered unwillingly, thinking she'd rather not live anywhere near this person.

'All taken, and good riddance!' the large lady snapped, and slammed the door in her face so hard that the stained-glass panels shook in their frames.

'How very rude,' Lily said, her cheeks burning pink as she came back down the steps. 'They can't all be that horrible – how would they ever get any lodgers?'

But it seemed they could. The next lodging-house keeper accused them of being runaways, and threatened to send for the police. They got almost as far as walking through the front door of the third house they tried, when the fussy, frilly woman who owned it spotted Henrietta sidling around Lily's ankles, and practically had a fit.

'You'd think she'd never even *seen* a dog,' Lily muttered crossly as they stalked away. 'You aren't dirty in the slightest, Henrietta, and don't believe anyone who says that you are.'

The next house was rather less attractive than some of the others. The card in the window had curled at the edges, and the muslin curtains were an unpleasant greyish shade. The bell didn't work either, so Lily hammered on the door. She was feeling militant now, and weary, and utterly starved. It was turning purplish dusk already, and she had no desire to be out on the streets with nowhere to sleep. They had seen several sad little bundles of rags on the omnibus journey, beggars and street people, and a fear of joining them was gnawing at her insides. She might have been neglected all her childhood, but she'd had a bed, and warmth, and food, even if it was haphazard and mostly flung at her by a grumpy cook. She had never been truly hungry, and from the look of those children, they were so hungry they'd almost stopped caring.

The door opened eventually, and a little old woman peered around it, and smiled at them toothlessly. Lily smiled uncertainly back. It was the friendliest welcome they'd had so far, but the old woman reminded her of the colour plates in a battered book of fairy tales that had been propping up a washstand in the rose-pink spare bedroom. If this wrinkled specimen offered her a bright-red apple, Lily decided, she wasn't going to risk it, however hungry she was.

'Er, do you have any rooms available?' she asked hesitantly.

'Of course, dear, of course! Walk this way. And your sister? And the sweet little dog too… Do come in…' The woman's voice was strangely slurred – because of her lack of teeth, Lily assumed.

She beckoned to Georgie and Henrietta, who were waiting at the bottom of the steps – after the last few houses, they had stopped bothering to come to the door.

'It isn't very clean,' Georgie whispered, as they followed the old woman into the house. It smelled of boiled fish, and cats, and their feet clung tackily to the linoleum as they walked down the hallway after her.

Henrietta sneezed, and stared up at Lily doubtfully.

'Dear little thing!' The old lady leered, and bent down to stroke the pug's head, but Henrietta dived behind Lily, with the merest whisper of a growl. Lily could understand – the woman's shawl reeked of some horrible sweet smell as she came closer, and there was dirt in the wrinkles round her neck.

'I'm sorry, she's rather shy,' Lily explained, and the growl got a little louder.

'Never mind, never mind. Now dears, such young ladies as yourselves, I do hope you don't mind me asking, but do you have the rent?'

'Oh yes,' Lily told her, her hand going unconsciously to the pocket of her dress.

The old woman's eyes followed it, and she smiled a sickly sort of smile, her eyes glinting.

'No. It's dirty, and she's a thief. Not here.'

'Dirty! The cheek! It most certainly is not!' the old woman cried, throwing up her hands. Then she glared suspiciously at the girls. 'Who said that?' she asked, her faded blue eyes wavering from one to the other.

'I'm so sorry! My sister, she's a little simple,' Lily explained, backing away. 'I'm afraid we've decided it won't suit. We – er – need rooms closer to the station. I'm sorry to have troubled you.' She turned, scooped up Henrietta, and raced for the door, feeling the old woman's hands clawing after her, and the drunken shriek of rage following them down the hallway, so potent and gin-laden that its fumes made her stagger.

Georgie fought the door-latch open, and they raced helter-skelter down the steps and along the street, until they could no longer hear her screaming. Then Lily ducked into a doorway, panting.

'So much for being discreet and hiding our magic and NOT TALKING!' Georgie snarled at Henrietta.

The pug did have the grace to look ashamed, ducking her head guiltily. 'She was a thief. She would have taken our money while we slept, and probably poisoned us too. She was a drunkard, and a witch as well.'

Lily lifted the little dog up to look properly into her face. 'She can't have been! Magic isn't allowed. I keep worrying that some of ours will seep out and we'll be caught. How can she be a witch?'

Henrietta tutted at her irritably. '*You* are a magician, clearly! And so is your sister! Do you think you're the only ones hidden? She threw a spell after us as we ran, but she was so befuddled with drink that it hardly touched us.'

'Oh,' Lily said blankly.

'It's so dark,' Georgie murmured. 'Where are we?'

'That's the British Museum, that big building over there with the columns. I've been there with Arabel. The girls' governess was very keen on it. She said it was most instructive. Although there were some bits of the statues that she wouldn't let them see.'

'Will it still be open?' Lily asked. 'It's all lit up. Perhaps we could go there, and – and think about what to do.' She didn't want to admit that she found the dark streets threatening. The blackness seemed so much worse here in the city, even though it was lit here and there with the golden glow of the gas lamps.

They hurried across the road, through a gloomy courtyard, and up the steps, vanishing between the massive stone columns, and into the shadowy caverns of the museum itself.

'It's like a palace,' Lily murmured, staring around at the high, coffered ceilings, and the statues gazing down forbiddingly from their pediments. She had often imagined that Queen Sophia must live in some grim, rich sort of place like this. One old gentleman was reading the inscriptions on a stone tablet, but otherwise the main entrance hall seemed to be empty, apart from the uniformed guards.

Georgie was standing in front of one of the dark red walls, looking at the delicately painted lettering and the little hands pointing to the various exhibits. 'Medals and coins, Zoological galleries, Egyptian rooms, Roman antiquities, the Elgin galleries…Exhibit of Forbidden and Treasonous Artefacts?'

'Let's go and see that. And quickly, because that guard over there is staring at us. I'm not sure dogs are allowed.' Lily hurried off down the corridor, with Henrietta skittering at her heels.

The treasonous artefacts, whatever they were, seemed to be something the museum was rather ashamed of. The corridors grew steadily narrower, grubbier and darker, and when they eventually found the gallery, it was dusty and poorly lit.

It only added to Lily and Georgie's feeling that they had come home.

They slipped in through the door – which bore a sign over the lintel saying *Bequest of Lady Amaranth Sowerby* – and gasped. The gallery was filled with display cases, shelves and pedestals, all packed with magical books and apparatus.

'Hmf.' Henrietta stared around her. 'This Lady Amaranth must have given the museum a great deal of money. They would never have put all this on show otherwise. It explains why it was so hard to find.'

'We've got one of those at home,' Georgie said, pointing at a tall glass vessel, painted with intricate designs in blue and gold. 'It's bigger than that one though.'

'Have we?' Lily eyed it thoughtfully. 'Oh! You mean that big flower vase in the passage upstairs?' She leaned over to read the card on the wall. 'Apparently it's an apparatus for infusing water with the smoke of infernal spirits,' she said doubtfully.

'Rubbish.' Georgie peered at the label. 'What on earth would you want to do that for?'

'So you can enter into a pact with the creatures of the underworld, it says so.' Lily giggled. 'You sprinkle the water in the shape of a five-pointed star and it traps the hell-beast inside. That's the silliest thing I've ever heard!'

'I don't think even Mama ever tried to trap a hell-beast.' Georgie sniggered.

'Your mother *is* a hell-beast,' Henrietta called from the other side of the gallery, where she was sniffing at a delicately embroidered cloak, displayed on a mannequin whose face was painted to look like some sort of evil clown.

'They've got everything wrong,' Georgie muttered crossly, as she wandered down between the cases. 'And look, that isn't a mandrake at all! You can see it's just stuck together out of bits of old tree root.' She stopped to read the label, and went white, stepping back from the case in horror. 'That's disgusting! How could they even think...? No, you aren't to read it,' she snapped, pushing Lily away.

'I don't need to, I've read some of the others,' Lily

said grimly. 'Georgie, is this what everyone thinks we are? People who murder children, and drink their blood?'

'That actually did happen,' Henrietta nudged her leg almost apologetically. 'Well, nearly. You were looking at the Sparrow bowl, weren't you? She was a distant cousin of yours, actually. Arabel's mother was mortified when it all came out. But Alethea Sparrow was mad! A great magician, obviously, but a complete madwoman with it. If you believed all of this, you'd think all magicians spent their days conjuring spirits and setting them to prey on the innocent.'

'But maybe that's what everyone else in the country does think,' Lily murmured, running her fingers over the sigils on the glass vessel. They tingled pleasantly. 'I hadn't realised quite what everyone thought of us. I mean, the servants were scared of Mama, but then so were we! Were they frightened of us too, all that time?'

Georgie blinked. 'I don't know. We had a nursemaid, a long time ago, but after she left I was with Mama all the time. I don't remember speaking to any of the servants very much after that.'

'They weren't. I'm sure they weren't... Martha was always giving me biscuits, and Violet was trying to teach me to write nicely. And Peter wasn't scared, or why would he have helped us to escape?'

'Perhaps he was too scared not to,' Georgie pointed out. 'Maybe he thought you'd turn him to dust if he didn't do as he was told. Oh, Lily, I didn't mean it,' she added quickly, as Lily's face crumpled. 'He was worried about you. And he certainly didn't need to meet us in the gardens last night, did he?' She frowned. 'Our servants had been at Merrythought a long time, most of them. They'd become accustomed, I think. We were real people, not the ogres the people who wrote this nonsense were imagining.'

'So anyone who hasn't been around magicians really thinks of us as monsters like this?' Lily asked in a small voice. Her dreams of restoring magic to England seemed even sillier now.

'And murderers. Regicides, even – it was a magician who killed the king, remember. If you ask me, it must have been mostly money that kept your servants there,' Henrietta said. 'High wages, and a little polite blackmail, for when those inspectors you mentioned were on their way. I'll bet all the servants got a bit extra then.'

Georgie nodded, but Lily had to swallow tears. She had thought they at least liked her. A little.

A damp nose nudged her hand. 'But remember Peter, Lily. I watched him as we rowed away. His eyes were glittering in the moonlight, and he stared after you for as long as I could see.'

EIGHT

'There's a bell ringing,' Georgie said, looking up anxiously. 'The museum must be closing. What are we going to do?'

Lily sat down on the corner of one of the pedestals, which held an ugly gold tripod that she strongly suspected was actually just a flowerpot-stand, and not the equipment for a conjured fire as its label claimed. 'Let's just stay here. Look how dusty everything is. I shouldn't think anyone will come and check. And there are lots of places to hide if they do. Then we can go and look for lodgings again tomorrow.' She sighed. She wasn't looking forward to it.

'When you said before that you couldn't manage a glamour in the middle of the street,' Henrietta asked

Georgie, 'did that mean that in a nice private space like this you could conjure one?'

Georgie frowned. 'I *have* done them. Only small ones. But I know how.'

Henrietta nodded. 'Then I suggest that tomorrow, before we leave here to go house-hunting, you change. Make yourselves look like old ladies, perhaps. No one would accuse a pair of elderly ladies of being runaways. It might be less difficult to find a room.'

'Won't it be easier if I help too?' Lily agreed eagerly. 'The spell to tidy us up worked well, didn't it? Teach me how to make the glamour, Georgie, please.'

'We can try,' Georgie said doubtfully. 'But last time I only changed the colour of my shoes, and even that gave me the most dreadful headache. Making both of us old might kill me.'

Henrietta simply stared at her, and Georgie gave a sulky sigh. 'Oh, very well! But if it all goes wrong, remember this was your idea!' She grabbed Lily's hand, and pulled her over into the corner of the gallery, sitting down on the floor with a decided flounce.

'This is going to take a lot of our power, Lily. You need to use all your magic. Can you remember how it felt when you pulled Henrietta out of the portrait? That must be the biggest spell you've done so far, I think.'

Lily shook her head, looking up at Georgie worriedly.

'I didn't mean to do it – it happened. Henrietta did it, not me.'

'I most certainly did not.' Henrietta came to sit in front of them, her tongue sticking out a little. It made her look very earnest, and rather silly. 'You called me. I don't have any magic. I *know* a lot about it, from living with Arabel. But you brought me out of that picture all by yourself, and you made it so I could talk – you said that you wanted someone to talk to, didn't you?'

'You really didn't mean to?' Georgie asked, leaning forward to scan Lily's face anxiously.

'No!' Lily felt like crying. She was useless after all.

'Unconscious magic, then...' Georgie shook her head, her eyes dark and round. 'That's the most powerful of all.' Then she let out a funny, half-bitter little laugh. 'It looks like Mama finally got what she wanted. You're the one they were trying to breed, Lily. A natural.'

'Don't be angry with me,' Lily said pleadingly.

'I'm not.' Georgie squeezed her hand. 'I think I'm nervous more than anything. There must be so much magic inside you, Lily. I'm a bit worried that it might all spill out. The wrong way.'

'What does that mean?' Lily demanded, her heart jumping fearfully.

Georgie shrugged. 'Absolutely no idea. But we ought to be able to manage a glamour, anyway.' She seized

Lily's hands, and sat with her eyes closed, breathing slowly, her teeth biting into her underlip. Henrietta wriggled close to Lily, and leaned on her. She looked up, and bared her teeth a little in a disturbing sort of grin. 'I like to feel the magic. It's buzzy.'

Lily nodded, and watched Georgie, feeling strangely nervous. She had no idea how a glamour spell worked, and she wasn't sure she wanted to change the way she looked.

'Lily!' Georgie opened her eyes and glared. 'You're blocking the spell. Stop it!'

'I didn't mean to...' Lily shook herself, trying to dislodge the fear and let the magic work. She could feel Georgie trying now, the magic prickling her skin, making the little hairs stand up on her arms.

'Breathe, Lily...' Henrietta growled in her ear.

Lily gulped. She had forgotten. She sucked in air, gasping, and suddenly Georgie's magic washed over her as if she'd breathed it in. Her eyes widened as she felt her own power dancing to meet it. When she had helped with the tidying spell, she had felt a little strange, as though she had pins and needles all over. This was different; strong and real – and wonderful.

Georgie was chanting again, but Lily could hardly hear the words, she was so caught up in the whirling dance of the magic in her veins. Then she felt a strange, aching shimmer all over, and her skin crawled on her bones. Fascinated and horrified, she stretched out her fingers in front of her, and they were no longer hers. They were an old lady's fingers, bony and gnarled, and clad in old-fashioned fingerless lace gloves. Lily stared at them for a moment, and then lifted them to her face, stroking the sagging flesh of her cheeks, and the folds under her chin.

Henrietta was looking between them, her little mouth gaping. 'So quick,' she muttered at last. 'And complete to a shade. Even the clothes. The little lace shawl crossed over your chest like that, Lily. And the cameo brooch! Georgie, you look like Arabel's grandmother, it's quite disturbing. She did not like dogs.'

Georgie was smirking proudly, an odd expression on the face of a seventy-year-old woman. 'Would you let out lodgings to us now, Lily?' she asked, her voice high and quavering, yet strangely still her own.

Lily shuddered, but nodded. 'How long will it last?'

Georgie's wrinkled face twisted, as though she were in pain. 'I'm holding on to it,' she explained. 'You have to keep it going, in the back of your mind, all the time. If I go to sleep, it'll wear off.'

'Well, you can't stay awake all night. Not after last night, when we hardly slept either. We know we can do the spell now, so can't we just do it again tomorrow?'

Georgie looked at her regretfully, like a painter being asked to spoil her masterpiece. 'You're sure you can help me recast it tomorrow?' she demanded.

'I think so.' Lily closed her eyes for a moment, and fumbled for the magic inside her. It was the oddest feeling. The magic seemed always to have been there, without her knowing what it was. Now that she recognised it, it wasn't hard to find – it leaped eagerly into her eyes and her mouth and her fingers as she came looking for it, and she laughed from pure pleasure as it glittered inside her.

'Lily, you're shining, stop it,' Henrietta hissed.

'Oh! I didn't realise I was doing it outside too!' Lily looked down at her fingers, and they were her own again, but now they glowed and sparkled and shimmered as she turned them admiringly this way and that. 'Is it a bad thing to do?' she asked Henrietta and Georgie worriedly. She liked it.

'No, only rather obvious,' Henrietta muttered uncomfortably. 'And it just looks wrong. I don't like it, Lily, put it out.'

'I think I remembered it from the light spell you made last night,' Lily explained, but Georgie grimaced. 'Mine was never that...extravagant. Doesn't it make you feel tired?'

Lily shook her head. 'It feels wonderful,' she whispered. She shook her hands, and the light scattered away like little dancing dust motes, which floated twinkling around the room. Lily blinked as she watched a few glittering sparkles land on a large stuffed crocodile, hanging in metal bands from the ceiling. It was a sad, faded-looking thing, its scales flaking away from age and neglect, but as the light shimmered over it, it seemed to twitch, and old, long-rotted muscles flexed under the skin, before it sank into sleep again. Lily looked down at her fingers nervously.

'We should go to bed,' Henrietta said firmly. 'I'm not used to all this gallivanting about. Pull some of those old robes at the back of the gallery down here, Lily, and we'll pile them up in this corner, out of sight of the door. Not that I think anyone will do more than steal in to put out the lights – if they even get that far.'

Lily nodded. Until the rush of magic had swallowed her up, she had been desperately hungry, but now her empty stomach was only a vague irritation, tucked away behind the sparkle of the magic still inside her.

Lily heaved the heavy, gold embroidered cloaks from the mannequins, half sneezing at the clouds of dust that she disturbed, and Georgie borrowed a pinch of yellowish powder from a little earthenware pot, and sprinkled it lavishly around their hiding place, muttering soft, secretive words to turn any prying eyes away.

Then they slept, curled in a nest of scratchy velvet, and safely surrounded by the things of home.

The light filtered through the small high windows slowly, and the girls woke late, to find Henrietta sitting in front of them looking grumpy.

'Did you scratch me?' Lily asked, rubbing her foot.

Henrietta ignored the question majestically, and fixed accusing eyes on Lily. 'When you have a dog, there are certain things you have to learn. One of which is the importance of regular mealtimes. In the last sixty years, all I have had to eat is six biscuits, and they were stale. We need to go and find me some food. You too, probably.'

'I gave you half of everything Martha gave me, the day we ran away!' Lily protested. But there hadn't been much to share. Now that Henrietta mentioned it, the magic that had subdued her hunger yesterday had settled down, and she was starving again.

Georgie looked as though she didn't mind as much. She was running her fingers through her hair and humming to herself, and the more she hummed, the glossier the hair became.

'That's your fault,' Lily muttered to Henrietta. 'She never bothered about it before.'

'Good.' Henrietta nodded approvingly. 'Care of one's coat is very important. But in this case, useless.' She nipped at Georgie's sleeve. 'Remember the glamour. It looks very nice now, but no one will see it.'

Georgie sighed. 'Yes. But I'll know it's nice underneath. It's like wearing your best petticoat, isn't it?'

Lily stared at her doubtfully. She only had two petticoats, and neither of them were nice enough to be called best. Georgie seemed to realise this suddenly, for she flushed pink, and hugged her. 'Let's do the glamour, and then we can go and get something to eat. I'm hungry too. I'm just used to it – Mama had breakfast in bed, so I never got anything before lunch. Hold my hands again.'

'We should put these away first. I'm sure I was shorter as an old lady, I don't think I could reach. Do you think anyone will notice they're a bit crumpled?' Lily shook out a gold and red silken affair worriedly. Then she glanced around the dusty gallery and smiled sadly. 'No, I suppose not.'

Georgie swept the ring of yellow powder away to join the rest of the dust on the floor, and then they stood in the middle of the gallery, hand in hand, to cast the glamour again. This time Lily searched for her magic eagerly, sending it out to join Georgie's, and trying to remember the words Georgie had spoken the night before. There was the same odd shimmering feeling as her skin shrivelled and changed, and in front of her Georgie was a stooped old woman again.

'Excellent,' Henrietta said. 'Now food, please. It feels late enough for the museum to be open, don't you think?'

Lily nodded. 'Yes. But won't they know they haven't seen us come in?'

Henrietta shrugged. 'Two little old ladies are hardly likely to have spent the night in the museum, are they? They will assume you slipped in when their backs were turned.'

Lily opened the gallery door, and peered out. No one was around, and they set off down the corridor, trying to walk slowly, rather than run as they really wanted to.

Eventually they emerged into the great hall, and Georgie led the way across the marble floor in a stately manner. She had furnished herself with a particularly impressive bonnet this time, for moral support, and a beribboned umbrella that Lily recognised as an imitation of the one the lady at Lacefield station had been carrying. The lace ruching on her bonnet nodded grandly as she stalked towards the doors, ignoring the two guards, who were watching them in puzzlement.

'Madam!'

Georgie had her hand on the door, and she cast

a desperate glance at Lily, clearly wondering if they should simply run.

Lily glared at her, and turned with a sweet smile to the approaching guard.

'Was there something?'

The man took off his hat, and Lily's smile deepened. She had been modelling her tone on Mama. 'Only that we didn't see you come in, ma'am…'

'But clearly we did…' Lily raised her eyebrows at him.

'We've only been open these last ten minutes…'

Lily glanced accusingly at Henrietta, and then nodded at the guard. 'Indeed. My sister and I came to see the – er –'

'Beetles!' Georgie put in hurriedly, and then went pink. 'Yes. We are most interested in beetles…' she added, her voice failing as she saw Lily rolling her eyes.

'But we couldn't find any, and so we are leaving.' Lily was poised to make a run for it, but the guard was nodding helpfully. 'Oh, yes indeed, ma'am. The beetles is all gone now, over to the new Natural History Museum, these last nine years.'

'Are they? Are they indeed?' Lily said gratefully. 'Well, it is some time since we have visited London. We're most grateful for your assistance. Come, Georgiana.' And she hurried Georgie and Henrietta out, before Georgie gave way to giggles entirely.

'Beetles! What were you thinking?' she hissed, as they pattered down the steps.

'I wasn't!' Georgie gasped, still laughing. 'I knew we had to say something, and I couldn't think of anything. Beetles just came into my head. And I was right, anyway!'

'We were lucky, you mean,' Lily said severely. 'Come on. Let's find something to eat.'

They were hurrying out along the street now, unsure which way to go, but simply eager to be away from the museum. At last they emerged from the warren of little streets onto a main road, already busy with carriages, and full of people.

'It's all very well, all these shops,' Lily murmured, licking her lips in front of the window of a baker's. 'But we can hardly buy a cake and eat it in the street.'

'Oh, Lily, look! Over there. Little tables, and there are other ladies sitting at them. Can't we go there?'

At the corner of the road was a smartly painted shop, with large plate-glass windows, and *Aerated Bread Co.* in large letters above them. Neat white-clothed tables filled the inside, and a girl about Georgie's age was pouring tea for a pair of middle-aged ladies.

Most unfortunately, in the window was a small notice, reading *NO DOGS*.

Henrietta's jowls drooped. 'Oh, and a cup of tea was exactly what I wanted,' she whispered in Lily's ear. 'What? Am I not allowed to like tea? Arabel used to put it in a saucer for me.'

'Could you hide in one of the bags, and we could feed you under the table?' Lily suggested tentatively, not sure if this undignified suggestion would get her bitten.

'Oh, very well,' Henrietta muttered ungraciously. 'But don't make a habit of it.' Lily quickly undid her bag, and Henrietta burrowed her way in. 'Don't do it up too tightly!' a small voice murmured from inside, as they pushed the door open.

There was a buzz of polite chatter, and a clinking of teacups, and Lily sighed happily at the delicious smells coming from the back of the teashop. Suddenly she was so hungry it was almost painful.

'We didn't make our hats big enough,' Georgie muttered, as they sat down at a little round table in the window, and a girl bustled over to serve them. 'Look at that one!'

Lily wrinkled her nose. 'It's got a bird in it, Georgie. That's just silly. Er, tea, please. And toast,' she added to the waitress. She wasn't sure what else to ask for – her breakfast was almost always bread and cheese, or a bowl of porridge eaten in the kitchen, while Mrs Porter glared at her, and arranged a delicate tray for Violet to carry up to Mama.

The carpet bag at her feet wriggled furiously, and whined. The waitress looked around in confusion, and Lily had to fake a coughing fit. The waitress hurried off to fetch a glass of water, and Lily kicked the bag – very gently.

'Shh!' Georgie hissed, leaning down as if she was fussing with her umbrella.

'Bacon…' the bag moaned. 'Toast, honestly!'

'Thank you,' Lily took the glass of water, and sipped it, trying to look ladylike. Several of the other customers had turned to stare. 'Would you have any bacon?'

The bag sighed happily, and Lily tried not to snigger.

'I feel much, much better now,' Henrietta practically purred in Lily's ear. They had decided that in the busy streets it was best for Lily to carry her, after she had quite audibly told one hurrying gentleman that he was an idiot and a clodpole when he stepped on her paw. Luckily he had thought it was Georgie speaking, and had apologised quite profusely.

'So do I!' Lily agreed. 'Although you nearly gave us away.'

'It isn't breakfast without bacon,' Henrietta muttered. 'Fancy thinking I only wanted toast! Anyway.

Now we need to find somewhere to stay. I suggest that after our dismal failure yesterday, you allow me to sniff out somewhere respectable.'

'Can you do that?' Georgie whispered doubtfully.

'Of course I can!' the pug snapped back. 'It's easy. Lily, put me down. Oh, don't worry! I promise not to talk. Although if any more idiots step on me, I might bite.'

So the two old ladies followed the little black pug dog on a roundabout route through London, pausing occasionally for Henrietta to sniff her way thoroughly around a building, before she changed her mind.

'Haven't you found anywhere yet?' Georgie hissed some time later, pretending to poke at a leaf with the point of her umbrella, so she could talk to Henrietta. 'I'm sure we've been down this street twice!'

'I know. We came back, because I wasn't sure, but now I am. Yes, this smells very good,' Henrietta looked up at the tall sugar-white building they were walking past.

'But this is a theatre, not a lodging house!' Lily drew into the shadows of an archway and pretended to examine a poster for a variety show. 'We can't live here!'

'It smells right,' Henrietta insisted stubbornly.

'Shh!' Lily hissed. Two men were coming out of the main door of the theatre, clearly in the middle of an argument. One of them had a bunch of keys in his hand, and a rolled-up poster under his arm, and he unlocked the poster frame in the niche on the other side of the door to theirs, while the other man went on shouting at him.

'We can't do it, Daniel! We'll all be arrested.'

'And think what wonderful publicity that would be,' the man with the poster pointed out. He was much younger than the other one, and extremely tall and thin. He was able to pin the poster into the top of the frame only by standing on tiptoe. He smoothed it out admiringly, and smiled, while his plump companion seethed next to him.

'Look! It practically says that it's real magic!' the little fat man wailed. 'The Queen's Men will be round by the end of the day.'

'It very carefully *doesn't* say that.' Daniel locked the frame again. 'It only hints. Broadly. It'll make us a fortune, Neffsky! Stop fussing. Besides, it's my act, if anything goes wrong, the rest of you can deny all knowledge, and see me led off to the magicians' cells.'

Lily peered out of her alcove, trying to read the poster. But all she could see was a black and white drawing of a man in evening dress, surrounded by what looked like rabbits, which she was sure couldn't be right. Rabbits had nothing to do with magic. She craned her neck further, and managed to read the curly black lettering. '*The Amazing Danieli will amaze you with his fantastical illusions...*' she whispered.

Neffsky turned round, and stomped back inside the theatre, still muttering angrily. Daniel waited until he'd gone inside, glanced around quickly, and then took two enormous strides and caught Lily's arm, making her squeak in horrified surprise.

'Off to fetch the Queen's Men, were we? Well, you can give them a message from me.' His voice was gruff, but Lily felt certain that was half put on. Close up, he looked even younger than she'd thought, only three or four years older than Georgie, she was sure. 'Tell them—'

'Lily!' Georgie dashed after her, and Henrietta barked furiously, harrying Daniel's ankles. 'Leave her alone, let go of her, you beast!'

In her fright, Georgie had let go of the glamour spell, and her face was changing even as she spoke. Lily felt her skin tighten over her bones, and glanced down to see her dress changing back to the pink muslin she had been wearing before the glamour took effect.

'What the...' Daniel was staring at them, his mouth half-open, then he suddenly glanced around the street, grabbed hold of Georgie too, and dragged them both inside the theatre.

NINE

Lily struggled violently as the tall boy, Daniel, hauled them along. She had a vague picture of gilt, and red velvet, and double doors under a sweeping staircase, leading into a hall full of delicate gilt-and-red chairs. It was all seen in flashes, as she pulled and wriggled, and tried to free herself.

'Stop it,' Daniel snapped, as she tried to bite his wrist. 'You little hell-cat!'

'Let go of me then! And stop hurting my sister. Look at her, she's fainting! Georgie, Georgie, what is it? Get off me, you!' Lily pulled, and then flung herself at Daniel's legs, and at last he let go of her with a grunt, clearly worried he was going to drop her sister. Lily found herself thankful for his manners.

One did not drop young ladies.

Georgie was lying collapsed against Daniel's arm. Her eyes had rolled up in her head, so that only the whites were showing, and her skin had paled to about the same colour.

The boy looked down at her in horror. 'What's the matter with her?' He was holding Georgie with both hands now, and he carried her over to another little velvet chair, and laid her down in it, fanning her face with one hand.

Lily pushed him out of the way and seized Georgie's hands, chafing them anxiously, and calling to her, but there was no response.

Henrietta jumped up onto the next chair, and sniffed Georgie crossly. 'She'll be perfectly all right. It's all nerves. You, pick me up.' This was addressed to Daniel, who obeyed her, looking as though his morning had gone very, very wrong.

'Hen-ri-etta!' Lily hissed. 'What are you doing? You're talking!'

'Oh for heaven's sake, Lily! The man has seen *you* transform from an old lady into a ten-year-old. He's hardly going to balk at a talking dog.'

'It is a little surprising still,' Daniel said meekly.

'Really?' Henrietta put her paws on his shoulder, and examined his face closely, sniffing his ears with careful attention. 'Clean linen,' she noted approvingly. 'And nicely trimmed ear hair. You can trust him, Lily. Though you missed a spot shaving this morning, just here, did you know?'

'Sorry, I haven't been doing it that long…'

'Hmm. Anyway, Lily, he's certainly trustworthy. Besides, he's a magician too, we saw the poster.'

'Oh, no, I'm not. My magic is all tricks,' Daniel explained, and Lily thought there was a wistful note in his voice. 'Designed to deceive an audience from a distance. You – you're real magicians? Aren't you?' His voice was desperately hopeful. 'Are you a girl in disguise too?' he added, staring at Henrietta.

'I most certainly am not!' Henrietta snapped. 'Why does everyone assume I'm something other than a dog?'

'So you do tricks with all those rabbits?' Lily asked. The rabbits had intrigued her.

Daniel blinked. 'Artistic licence. There are actually only two rabbits. But they are white ones, and very well trained.'

'What have rabbits got to do with magic?' Lily frowned, but Daniel was no longer looking at her.

'Hey! I don't think you should be waving that around! Miss, please!'

Georgie had come out of her trance, and was sitting up straight on her chair. But she was as white-faced as ever, and her eyes were blazing an unnatural jewel-like blue. The fire in them was made even brighter by the reflection of the white fireball she was nursing between her hands. She seemed to be poised to hurl it at Daniel.

'Georgie, don't! Henrietta says we can trust him!' Lily cried.

But Georgie didn't even seem to hear her. She stood up jerkily, turning the ball of flame over in her hands. Despite their brightness, her eyes seemed blank, as though there was no Georgie behind them. She cupped the ball of fire closer, and seemed to smile as its heat flushed her cheeks a little. And then she threw it, straight at Daniel.

He stood there, aghast, as Georgie crumpled slowly to the ground, and Lily and Henrietta raced to save him. The fireball flew through the air, and Henrietta leaped after it, batting at it with just the tip of one outstretched paw, and howling.

The flames seemed to stall in midair for just a second, long enough for Lily to seize it, scream as the white flames blistered her fingers, and hurl it through the double doors into the theatre, where it collided with one of the little velvet chairs and exploded.

'Did it burn you? Lily, show me! It singed my claws, it must have burnt you.' Henrietta tugged Lily's skirt angrily with her teeth. 'Show me!' Her voice was rising to a howl.

'It's all right,' Lily said weakly, crouching down and opening her hands to show the little dog. 'I thought it had too – it felt as though it had. But there aren't any marks. It's Georgie's magic – maybe it doesn't hurt me in the same way it would someone else. It probably would have crisped you,' she added wearily to Daniel, who was stooping over Georgie, looking anxious.

'She's fainted again.'

'Making quite a habit of it,' Henrietta muttered. She stalked over to Georgie, and licked her face lavishly.

'Is that hygienic?' Daniel murmured shakily, but then he shut his mouth with a snap when Henrietta turned round and eyed him meaningfully.

Georgie twisted and moaned, and then started to sit up. 'Oh, you didn't...' she murmured, wiping a wobbly hand across her face. 'Lily, did you let her...'

Lily glared at her. 'I can't believe you're cross with me! Georgie, you nearly killed him! And who knows how much of our gold buying a new chair will take!'

'What are you talking about? Why do we need a chair? I have the most dreadful headache,' Georgie whispered, pressing her hands to the sides of her head.

'You deserve one! You don't even know you did it,

do you?' Lily yelled at her furiously. 'You threw a ball of fire at him! You exploded a chair!'

'I'm sure I did not!' Georgie folded her arms, and glared, but then she saw the way Daniel was eyeing her, and her mouth trembled. 'I didn't... How could I do that and not remember?'

'You did look strange,' Lily admitted. 'Like you did that time you were sleepwalking years ago, do you remember? The same odd look in your eyes – they were open, but you weren't really seeing anything.'

'She smells different,' Henrietta hissed to Lily, in a secretive sort of whisper that she clearly meant everyone to hear. 'A musky sort of smell. Like your mother's magic.'

'Listen,' Daniel was glancing around anxiously. 'You'd better come into my office – this is my theatre, you see. I inherited it, last year, from my uncle. We can't have this sort of conversation out here. There are rehearsals going on – we're lucky the sword-swallowers are out in the back yard having a row, or they'd have seen your little chair-exploding incident. I shall have to say I was experimenting with some new pyrotechnics for my act.' He sighed. 'They'll believe that, they all think I'm only a deluded child anyway. Come on. Safer in here.' He took Georgie's arm, and led her to a door tucked away in one corner of the hall.

Daniel's office was a tiny little room, which seemed to be used to store everything that people couldn't find a place for anywhere else. Lily heaved a tigerskin rug off one of the chairs, and Henrietta sat down nose to nose with it, admiring the teeth.

'Who *are* you?' Daniel asked, sweeping a pile of papers onto the floor, and sitting down on the edge of his desk.

Lily and Georgie exchanged glances. How much did they trust Henrietta's judgement? How much should they tell him? He was obviously interested in magic, even if his own was all faked. But if he was too interested, he might be able to tell someone where they were.

Lily sighed. They'd already destroyed one of his chairs, not to mention trying to kill him. And he had a trustworthy sort of face. 'Lily and Georgiana Powers,' she told him, burrowing her hand into Georgie's.

'Powers? I've read about you!' Daniel's eyes lit up. 'The same family as Alethea Sparrow! The – er – blood-drinking one... You live in that house on the island, off the Devon coast somewhere.'

'Merrythought? You've read about us?' Lily asked curiously.

Daniel nodded. 'You're one of the old families. I've read up on all of them. Actually, I didn't know there were any Powers left.' He shook his head, his eyes shining. 'I can't believe it. That was a glamour! I've *seen* a glamour!'

Georgie shivered. 'I suppose we've been shut up on the island, since the Decree. Hardly anyone would know.'

Daniel nodded. 'And the Queen's Men like it that way, I'll bet. So…are you living in London now?' he asked hopefully. He looked like a little boy in a sweet shop. Lily could tell he was desperate to see more magic. Real magic.

Henrietta sniffed. 'We'd like to be. It turns out it's rather difficult to find lodgings for two girls and a dog.'

'Look…' Daniel frowned, obviously thinking hard. 'Our new variety show opens next week, and The Amazing Danieli – that's me – has top billing. Perk of owning the theatre, though I'm beginning to think it was some sort of midsummer madness. The rest of the acts aren't happy, they think we're going to get into trouble, and frankly, just now no one thinks the act is good enough. It needs something different. Something extra.' He gave Lily a sideways, hopeful glance.

'Three rabbits?' she suggested innocently. Daniel ignored her.

'If I let you live here, couldn't you help me with the act somehow?'

'Do you want to get arrested?' Henrietta demanded. 'Surely a magic show is asking for trouble as it is! Now you want it to look *more* authentic?'

Daniel nodded. 'Obviously we'd have to be very careful. But you could advise me, couldn't you? Suggestions? Everyone loves a little magic – or what looks like it.'

'But they don't!' Lily told him despairingly. 'We couldn't find anywhere to stay last night, and we ended up sleeping in the British Museum. In the Treasonous Objects exhibit. People don't love magic a bit, they think we're all mad murderers!'

Daniel shook his head. 'No. No, you see, that's the thing. All those magical objects were left to the museum by an old lady – she wasn't a magician, but she loved magic, and she'd collected all that stuff. Her family had some sort of magic shop, they made a lot of money out of it.'

'Some of it isn't anything to do with magic,' Lily pointed out. 'A lot of it was fake, and practically everything had the wrong labels.'

'All saying it was much nastier than it really is, I know. She left the museum a lot of money, that Lady Amaranth Sowerby. Millions. But they only got the money *if* they displayed her collection. So they did – but to keep the queen happy, they had to call it Treason. And they buried it all in the darkest corner they could find. I should think I'm the only person who ever visits, and I've only been twice – the museum guard recognised me. I don't want him tipping off the Queen's Men.'

'So people don't hate us quite that much?' Lily said slowly.

Daniel looked thoughtful. 'There's a lot of bad feeling about magicians still, I grant you that. With old Queen Adelaide – the widowed queen, you know – with her still going everywhere covered in black lace and jet jewellery, it's hardly surprising. But magic itself – the pretty things magicians used to do every so often, paper birds, the jewelled flowers. People remember that, and they miss it. Plus it's forbidden, so it's exciting, you see. That's the sort of thing I do in my act – beautiful, and a little bit scary. Exciting! But it could be so much better if I knew more about real magic.' He looked from Georgie to Lily, pleadingly. 'I could let you live at the theatre. It'd be an exchange.'

'You'd like Georgie to make a habit of throwing balls of fire into your audience?' Lily shook her head doubtfully.

'No, no, of course not. But dressed in the right sort of robe – she's very pale. We could pass her off as some sort of Nordic magical princess… Magic's not outlawed abroad, remember. She could assist me in the act. You both could! That would be better than rabbits, most definitely.'

'We're supposed to be hiding!' Georgie hissed. 'Not appearing on a stage in front of hundreds of people!'

'Hundreds might be a slight exaggeration,' Daniel sighed. 'Although if the new act is a success…'

'Why aren't you racing off to fetch the Queen's Men yourself?' Lily asked suddenly. 'Isn't it treason not to report us?'

Daniel shrugged. 'Not everyone believes that magic should be outlawed. One mad magician, and a whole race are driven underground? Hardly fair. I've read a lot of magical history, while I was planning the act – and even that could have me imprisoned, the rules are so strict. I had to do a lot of hanging around on street corners, buying books from men who didn't have names. But one of the things I realised was that magicians were very rich, and not very popular, even after the Talish invasion was driven back. Getting rid of them was a good move for Queen Sophia – or whoever it was advising her.'

'You sound like our mother,' Georgie said, and she shivered, and looked at Lily. 'Just a moment,' she murmured, pulling Lily aside, Henrietta trotting after them. 'I trust him…especially if I really did try to set him on fire. He may be rather – deluded – but we don't have much choice! Lily, we need someone who can help us. We don't know anything – remember how everyone stared just because we had no gloves? It's going to be like that all the time. If we try to keep going on alone, sooner or later we'll betray ourselves utterly.'

Lily frowned at Daniel. 'If we help you in this magic act, you'll really let us live here?'

Daniel nodded. 'There's a warren of back rooms behind the stage. I'm not saying it'll be luxurious, but it's warm.'

'I suppose it's the last place she'd think of looking for us.' Lily nodded.

Daniel frowned. 'Someone's looking for you?' he asked.

'Not the Queen's Men. Our mother. We've run away,' Lily admitted.

'What? Why?'

Lily shook her head. 'I don't think we can tell you that,' she murmured apologetically. 'We have to hide. That's all we can say.'

But Daniel didn't look satisfied. 'How old are you?' he asked Lily bluntly.

Lily swallowed. 'Ten,' she said quietly. 'Georgie's twelve,' she added, as though that made a huge difference.

'Ten...' Daniel sat down heavily. 'You really are

children. Your glamour – I was still half thinking you were older than me… And you've run away from home. No, this is wrong…'

'You aren't far off a child yourself.' Henrietta sniffed his trouser legs, and eyed him shrewdly. 'What are you, sixteen? Seventeen?'

Daniel reddened, and she nodded to herself. 'Thought so.'

'You're helping us, how can that be wrong?' Georgie seized his hands. 'We need you, and you need us! We ran away from our mother because she's using my magic.' She frowned. 'It's hard to explain. She wants me to do something bad.' She pulled away from Daniel, sitting back on her knees on the floor. 'She's spoilt my magic, I think… When I'm frightened, or angry, something else takes over. I really didn't mean to hurt you, sir,' she promised him earnestly. 'It wasn't me… You can't send us back to her, you see that, don't you?'

'But I'll be using you just as much as she was!' Daniel shook his head.

'It isn't the same at all!' Lily cried. 'You're helping. We're just helping you back.'

'And it isn't such a good bargain,' Georgie muttered. 'I will have to stop doing any magic at all.' She rubbed her hands wearily across her eyes. 'I was trying to keep the glamour going, and fight you off, sir. That's when whatever's buried in me started to work. If I don't let my magic loose, then no one can twist it out of my hands, can they?'

She sounded almost relieved, Lily thought. In fact, there was a faint smudge of a smile at the corner of her mouth. Lily watched her, the lines between Georgie's eyes smoothing away as she suddenly realised she needn't do any more magic. That she *mustn't*. Georgie looked happier than she'd ever seen her, Lily realised, starting to frown herself.

How could they be so different? Lily could still feel the prickling excitement of the magic lying just underneath her skin. She felt as though she had a candle flame hidden in her hand, and the light was shining through her fingers. Her magic was desperate to escape, and she wanted it to. She wanted it to dance and twirl and make fireworks. Her fingers itched to practise more spells. She remembered the words of her father's letter – she couldn't imprison her magic either.

Georgie laughed. 'You've never been made to do it, Lily. I can see you thinking how stupid I am.'

Lily shook her head quickly. 'No! It's only – how can you not want magic, when it feels like this?' She spread her fingers out, smiling to herself, and flexing the power inside her.

Georgie only shivered. 'It makes my skin crawl.

I think I'd prefer the pretend kind.'

'Are you sure?' Daniel asked, still frowning. 'You do want to do this?'

But when the girls looked at each other and nodded, his frown faded, and all of a sudden he laughed out loud. He sprang up, and grabbed Lily's arms, swinging her round in his excitement. 'We'll have the best act you can imagine. To think I was relying on those commonplace rabbits!' Then he set Lily down, and added, much more seriously, 'And if something should happen to...well, go *wrong*, you can simply blame it on the magic act. You were practising illusions, that's all. If you're known to be my associates, everyone will think your magic is faked, like mine.'

Georgie's smile grew even wider. 'Of course,' she murmured, with a breath of relief.

Henrietta sniffed. 'I have a distinguished pedigree, you know. Descended from champions. If I had known I was to become some sort of circus creature, I would have stayed in that painting.' But her tail was twitching, and her tongue was sticking out with excitement.

Lily knew exactly how she felt.

TEN

In the space of an hour, they had found both a home and a job, Lily realised, looking around the rather dusty room at the back of the theatre that Daniel had shown them into. It was a little smaller than her bedroom back at Merrythought, but she didn't care. Henrietta was certain that Daniel was to be trusted, and Lily believed her, even more so after he had promised them lunch. She was a little worried though. Daniel had been full of plans, as he hurried them through the passageways. And his plans sounded time-consuming. Rehearsals. Costume fittings.

When were they going to fit in finding Father? Still, the dark, close little room felt very safe. Who would look for them here? Mama and Marten would never suspect they were in a theatre. How could they be, when two days ago they'd hardly known such things existed?

Lily had no idea how Marten hunted – whether she was following their magic somehow, or simply sniffing them out like a dog. But here, surrounded by people, was surely a good place to hide? They would stay a while, she thought, gratefully. Only a little while, until they knew more about the world they'd escaped into. Then they'd set out searching.

'It'll be busier this afternoon,' Daniel explained back in the office, as he pulled out a loaf of bread, and a hunk of hard cheese for their lunch. 'Late nights mean theatre people often sleep late, even though the show doesn't open till next week. But after lunch more people will start to trickle in to rehearse.'

'What do you want us to do, in your act?' Lily asked. 'I've never seen a magic show – or been to a theatre, even, apart from this one. I don't know what happens.'

Daniel snorted. 'Most of the people in this country have never seen a magic show. It isn't exactly illegal, but it is a little, er, borderline. People will know it isn't real – how could it be, we'd be arrested. But it's got to look real. And people will wish that it was, you see, that's the important thing. Everyone loves a little bit of mystery. Just a little magic, at a nice safe distance.' He sighed.

'I hope so, anyway. You saw Neffsky arguing with me earlier on. He's convinced it's going to be a disaster.'

'Is he part of the show, too?' Lily asked.

Daniel nodded. 'He's a singer. We have all sorts – jugglers, contortionists, the sword-swallowers, although we may not have them for much longer. The act's getting to them, I think. They're fighting all the time, and when you spend a great deal of your life with a sword in various bits of you, it's dangerous to lose your temper. Then there's the ballet troupe, of course, and the Six Sandersons, they're trick cyclists.' He stopped, looking at Lily's blank face. 'You haven't the faintest idea what I'm talking about.'

'People *swallow* swords?' Lily asked him doubtfully. 'That seems even sillier than the rabbits.'

Daniel frowned and leaped up from the tigerskin rug, where he'd been sitting to eat his share of the bread and cheese. 'The rabbits are not in the slightest bit silly. I shouldn't have called them commonplace before. They're pure white, very expensive, actually.'

'I've never met a sensible rabbit,' Henrietta said, snatching the crust out of his hand, and bolting it. Then she stared at him smugly.

'Come and watch, come on! And you, quiet,' he added fiercely to Henrietta. 'The rest of the performers will be coming in. You all need to be careful.'

He led them into the main theatre, and trotted up a set of little steps onto the stage. 'Sit there,' he ordered, waving them into the front row of chairs. 'I just need to fetch everything. For the real performance, of course, everything will be all set out ready.'

Lily and Georgie curled themselves shyly into the chairs he'd pointed out, and watched wide-eyed. The theatre had filled up while they were eating sandwiches in the office. A knot of men in shirtsleeves were hauling painted screens up and down at the back of the stage, and arguing about something that had stuck, and exactly whose fault it was. Meanwhile a group of girls in filmy pink costumes were dancing in a line across the stage, their arms linked, and cleverly avoiding the scenery mechanism with a series of hops.

Daniel came back onto the stage, now wearing a top hat, and carrying a little table with a bright-red cloth on it, trimmed with bobbles. Mrs Porter had had something very like it in her sitting room back at the house, Lily remembered, with a sudden lurch inside. She wondered how angry Mama had been, after they ran away. Would she have revenged herself on the servants? Mrs Porter had always been bad-tempered and impatient, but then she had been like that with everyone. She'd given Lily raisins in twist of paper, and sometimes even sugar. Lily blinked away a film of tears, as she watched Daniel making odd gestures around the covered table. He appeared to be trying to show that it was definitely a table.

Then he swept the hat off his head, bowing elaborately to the audience. He came to the front of the stage, and wafted the hat about, turning it up so that they could see it was empty, swirling his hand around inside, and even tossing it into the air. 'Imagine that I'm wearing a long black cloak,' he hissed to them. 'It helps. And there's music too, very dramatic, eerie stuff. Mostly Fred on the violin.'

Lily nodded. Georgie was trying not to laugh, and Henrietta was sitting up on her chair, watching with an air of deep suspicion. Her tail was twitching, ever so slightly. Lily stroked her, and whispered, 'Whatever it is, don't talk!' Henrietta only glared.

Daniel strolled back to the table, putting the hat brim-down on the table, while he unfolded a white silk handkerchief, which he spread out on the table with a flourish. Then he placed the hat on the handkerchief, paused dramatically, and pulled a small, rather surprised-looking white rabbit out of the hat.

The dancers and stagehands, who'd obviously seen it several times before, seemed not even to notice, but Henrietta barked excitedly, standing up on her chair, and jumping around on all four paws. Lily and

Georgia clapped a little, out of politeness, and Daniel frowned. He came back down the steps towards them, affectionately cradling the rabbit.

'Didn't you like it?' he asked in a low voice. He looked rather hurt, and Georgie patted his arm encouragingly. 'It was very – nice. I'm sorry, it's just such a simple little spell,' she whispered. 'Lily could do it, and she hasn't been trained at all. Her magic really only started to work a few days ago.'

'But it isn't a spell!' Daniel hissed crossly. 'The rabbit was there all the time!'

Henrietta nodded excitedly, her tail practically vibrating.

'No, it wasn't.' Lily shook her head. 'You showed us – you held the hat upside down. The rabbit would have fallen out, even if you'd covered it up inside the hat.'

Daniel smirked. 'It was though. Not in the hat, exactly…'

'Back of the table.' Henrietta whispered it out of the corner of her mouth. 'Tipped it in when you turned the hat the right way up again.'

'Did you see?' Daniel asked her anxiously.

Henrietta shook her head a fraction. 'Smelled,' she murmured. 'Clever.'

'Well, if it wasn't real magic, I suppose it was rather

clever,' Lily admitted. 'Why a rabbit though? Why not a cat? Or – or a hedgehog?'

'Rabbits keep still,' Daniel explained. 'And they don't make any noise either. Imagine wrapping a cat up in a silk handkerchief, and hanging it off the back of a table for twenty minutes. Even if it didn't tip the table over, it would rip my hand to shreds as soon as I tried to pull it out of a hat.'

Henrietta snorted, but rather regretfully. She was eyeing the rabbit as if she envied it a little.

'You would be better than a rabbit,' Lily told her lovingly. 'Rabbits have no character.'

'Well, I think that's why it's funny. Bella just looks so innocent.' Daniel stroked the rabbit's ears gently, and it went on suspiciously eyeing Henrietta. 'A very clever dog, though… It's an interesting idea.' He stared at Henrietta thoughtfully. 'Until now, I've done all my tricks by myself, but the possibilities are endless if you have people working with you. I have the drawings for a cabinet – I tried to convince one of the dancers to hide in it and help me, but she was very suspicious of the whole idea.' He scowled gloomily. 'In fact, she said that I was mad, and she wasn't going to climb into any such instrument of the devil.' A smile curved the corner of his mouth, and he looked dreamy for a moment. 'It would be the most wonderful illusion. I thought of adding a sort of shadow play element, after she said that, so that there would appear to be great clawed hands…'

Lily sighed. 'Is it dangerous?'

'Oh no! Well…no. Only a little squashed,' Daniel admitted.

'If you promise to give us money for food, as well as the room, we'll do it. Advise you on the illusions, and climb out of cabinets. Won't we?' She nudged Georgie.

Georgie was chewing her hair again. 'No real magic?'

Daniel shook his head firmly. 'It's tempting, but…we mustn't.'

'Very well.' Georgie nodded.

'Who are you?' A girl the same age as Lily was standing in front of them, looking contemptuous. Daniel had promised to introduce them to some of the other theatre people, but he had gone to put Bella the rabbit away in her hutch, leaving Lily and Georgie to watch the rehearsals. 'This is private rehearsal time, you know. You can't simply walk in and sit down. Sam! There's a pair of country bumpkins sitting in the auditorium! Get rid of them!'

The man in charge of the stagehands, who had now managed to mend the scenery mechanism, and were practising the change from a Japanese water garden to a Talish forest, turned round. There was a set to his shoulders that made Lily think this sort of thing happened rather often. 'What is it, Miss Lydia?' he asked politely.

'I told you! Trespassers!' The girl pointed a finger dramatically at Lily, until Henrietta snapped at it. Then she reeled back shrieking, as the stagehands snorted with laughter. 'Somebody shoot it! It probably has hydrophobia!'

'Miss Lydia, these young ladies are part of Mr Daniel's new act.'

'And so is our dog,' Lily said sharply. 'And she isn't mad. You stuck your finger in her face, and she was very restrained – she didn't even touch you.'

Miss Lydia ignored this completely. Her expression had changed as soon as she heard that Lily and Georgie were part of the show. The contempt was still there, but now it was tinged with jealousy, and a hint of fear. 'You? Performers? Hardly, dressed like that.' She waved a hand to indicate their outdated dresses, and smirked nastily.

Lydia herself was wearing a miniature version of an adult's dress, floor-length, and tightly-laced. Her waist was tiny with the corset, and the huge bustle sticking out behind, but Lily thought she looked desperately uncomfortable. She was carrying a little frilled pink parasol, and her hat fountained pink feathers over her long, silvery-blonde curls.

'So what do you do? He can hardly pull you out of a hat.' Lydia laughed, a very artificial, musical little laugh on at least six notes.

'Ah! I see you've met!' Daniel hurried down the steps looking slightly anxious. 'Lily and Georgiana, this is Lydia Lacey.'

'The Little Silver Songbird.' Lydia fluttered her eyes closed in pretend modesty, clearly expecting them to be impressed. When they didn't say anything, she looked up crossly. 'My voice is famous. Even the royal family have heard of me.'

Lily smiled. The royal family had almost certainly heard of her too, but for different reasons.

'Mr Daniel! I hope you're going to clear the stage for Lydia to rehearse.' A large woman with very bright yellow hair, a colour that surely couldn't be quite natural, was bearing down on them. Despite her bulk, there was something about her round, greenish-blue eyes that made Lily sure the woman was Lydia's mother. Her dress was even more extreme than her daughter's, and she looked as though she might explode out of it at any moment. 'She needs perfect quiet – she can't possibly perform with all this going on.' She skimmed a glance over Lily and Georgie, and clearly decided they were not worth commenting on.

'Perhaps just this once – we are rather pressed for

time, with the grand re-opening next week,' Daniel began, but Lydia's mother seemed to inflate like an outraged pigeon, putting her dress at even more risk of bursting. He sighed. 'Lads! Down tools. Miss Lacey wishes to rehearse.'

'*Thank* you.' Lydia's mother bowed to him graciously.

Sam, the head stagehand, stomped down the steps and settled himself leaning against the front of the stage to talk to Daniel. He nodded at Lily and Georgie in a friendly sort of way, and then his gaze fell on Henrietta, and his eyes brightened.

'Lovely little thing, aren't you?' he cooed, holding out a hand for her to sniff.

Lily scowled meaningfully at Henrietta, but she needn't have worried. The little pug was practically simpering, rubbing herself around Sam's hand, and looking up at him adoringly.

'Goodness, she's never normally that friendly,' Lily said surprised.

The big man smiled, and shrugged. 'She's a little beauty. We've fixed that winch now, Mr Daniel.'

'Good, good. Sam, would one of the carpenters be able to knock me up a little something, for the act, do you think? A sort of folding cabinet, nothing too complicated... And talking of winches...'

Over the days that followed, almost everyone else in the theatre welcomed Lily and Georgie, especially after Daniel had carefully implied that they were some sort of distant cousins of his. One of the stagehands even told her that their act was proper clever. But Lydia and her mother lost no opportunity to be unpleasant. Lydia deliberately tripped Georgie in the wings, and tore her silver dress for the act. She had apologised sweetly, claiming it was an accident, but Henrietta had seen her quite clearly.

'She's jealous,' Henrietta had told them later that night, back in their little room. The sisters were sharing an old brass bed that Daniel had unearthed from somewhere. The mattress was lumpy, and had a slight odour of mouse – although it was only Henrietta who could really smell it – but they slept curled all three together, never missing their cold, dusty rooms back home.

'I don't understand why she's jealous of us,' Lily complained. 'She's the great singing star, with her sketch in the newspapers, and princes from all over Europe wanting her to come and entertain them. Or so she says.'

'She showed me the newspaper article,' Georgie admitted gloomily. 'It did say she had a wonderful voice, and that the audience was moved to tears.'

'Huh,' Lily muttered. 'But we don't sing. Why should she be so mean?'

Henrietta padded further up the bed to nestle on the counterpane in between the sisters. 'They are starting to see it, I think. I know you don't admire Daniel's tricks, but if you had no magic... If you'd never seen magic... They are impressive. And our little additions are masterly,' she added smugly. 'Georgie adds dramatic atmosphere. And Alfred Sanderson – he's the red-headed one who can play the violin while he's going backwards on the unicycle – said that I had natural comic timing.' She licked Lily's hand sympathetically. 'And you look very nice in your blue dress.'

Lily chuckled, and snapped her fingers at the candle to put it out. She didn't care if she wasn't the star of the magic act – she could do the real thing. But she'd hardly been able to do any magic over the last ten days, with all the rehearsals and dress fittings, and last-minute errands round the theatre. After years of being alone almost all the time, and feeling she was a nuisance whenever she did try to talk to someone, Lily felt as though she'd travelled to another world, far further than a train journey could have taken her. At last she seemed to be somewhere she was wanted. Henrietta was right, their act was good. Lily had noticed the reactions as they rehearsed, the stagehands and scene-painters gradually stopping their work to peer over at what they were doing. There was a hunger for magic, Lily could feel it. Or if not for magic, then just for something special and exciting. From what Daniel and the others had said, it wasn't only magic that Queen Sophia's Decree had suppressed. There seemed to be more rules about everything now, and theatres were always being inspected, in case they were showing something dangerous or improper. Everyone in the theatre seemed to hate the Queen's Men, just as Lily and Georgie had been brought up to do. Sam had even spat when Lily had mentioned them while she helped him hang a new piece of scenery. He'd then apologised, shamefaced, especially after Henrietta barked at him. He adored Henrietta, and he kept bringing her little treats, and feeding her the crust off his meat pie at lunchtime.

As soon as the wardrobe mistress, the stagehands and everyone else had realised that the girls were always there, and didn't mind being asked, they were constantly sent out for a pennyworth of scarlet thread, or a bag of nails, or even just the lighting man's lunch.

Georgie had befriended Maria, the wardrobe mistress, by admiring the costumes. Maria was so glad to have another pair of hands willing to sew sequins onto leotards that she showed Georgie how to alter a pair of old dresses for herself and Lily, so that they might have something a little more up-to-date – or at least only a couple of years behind the current fashion.

While Georgie was sewing and picking up gossip in the wardrobe, Lily and Henrietta had grown quite at home in the warren of little alleys that ran around the back of the theatre. Lily was still a little anxious about going further, though. Every so often she found herself out on the main streets for an errand, and it scared her. She felt like a leaf, tossed about on the waves at home, turned this way and that by the hurrying crowds. Perhaps she would get used to it, she had thought the first time, pressing herself back against the cold glass of a shop window, and gasping for breath.

She would have to. Lily frowned to herself in the darkness. The theatre was so exciting, so bright and warm, that it would be easy to forget why they'd had to run. They *had* almost forgotten, this past week, she realised. She couldn't be a conjuror's assistant for ever. But if they left the theatre, and the warren of little alleys around it, she was horribly certain that Marten would hunt them out. She and Georgie were supposed to be searching for their father, and that would mean venturing out of their safe cocoon.

How did one even find a magicians' prison? Would they be allowed to visit, or write a letter? If they had to use magic to find him, Lily suspected that would call Marten after them. She bit her lip, guiltily. They had to try harder – the glittery false magic of their act had made her forget the real kind. She smiled, feeling it leap inside her, the blood suddenly thundering in her ears. She couldn't hold it back. She dug her nails into her palms. If they had to get rid of Marten so Lily could set her magic free, and her father's, then they would. Somehow. Her magic surged around her blood, flinging itself eagerly against her skin. Lily frowned. If only she knew how to use it better. If they had to use Georgie's magic against Marten, more of Mama's strange spells might surface...

'I feel sick,' Georgie murmured.

She did look terribly white, Lily realised. 'You can't,' she hissed. 'We've been rehearsing this for a week, Georgie! It's us now, any minute, after Lydia finishes that awful song about the flowers growing on her mother's grave. I wish they were. Her mother said I looked like a charity child this morning.'

Georgie's eyes sparkled with fury, as Lily had hoped they would. 'Even in your new dress? How dare she! Especially when she looks like an elephant in pink frills!'

'Ready?' Daniel appeared beside them, looking anxious, and cradling Bella the rabbit, half-wrapped in the black silk handkerchief he used to hide her in behind the table.

'I think so,' Lily whispered. She was nervous too, although she didn't really have to do anything difficult, only the Demon's Cabinet, as she was smaller than Georgie. Her sister had turned out to have a surprising talent for dancing around the stage looking mysterious, which was apparently exactly what was needed. Her white-blonde hair had been decorated with a sparkly tiara, and she was wearing a silvery robe that looked a little like the ones the girls had slept on in the museum. She was to be introduced as a snow princess, from an icy Northland, full of ancient magic. Brownish hair seemed to disqualify Lily from being a snow princess, which she was rather glad about. She liked dancing, but she preferred the fast bouncy sort that the comic singers did, not the slow arm-waving kind that Georgie had copied from the ballet dancers. Georgie's soulful expression reminded Lily too much of the way she looked when she had a stomach ache.

Lydia was curtseying now, very beautifully, Lily admitted grudgingly to herself. She didn't like the bell-like way Lydia sang – it made her skull vibrate – but the audience certainly seemed to adore her. Several of them were even standing up to clap, and Lydia was still curtseying, and running back to the front of the stage again and again, with a sweetly modest expression on her face that made Lily clench her teeth. Daniel's act *had* to go well. She could feel her magic calling as she waited, little sparks fizzing inside her. But Lydia was on what must be her last curtsey by now. Lily shook herself, trying to squash the magic back down. It would be so easy to turn Bella into something more interesting inside that hat, she thought wickedly, as Lydia finally ran off into the wings. It would ease the giggly, tickling feeling of too much magic, cooped up inside her. But she banished the thought as the heavy velvet curtains swept together, and she hurried the cabinet to the back of the stage, then turned to smile and pose, as the curtains drew slowly open once more.

ELEVEN

Lily held her breath. If she breathed too deeply, the panels would ripple, and everyone, or at least those in the front rows of the audience, would be able to see where she was. She still found it hard to believe that no one could tell, once she was safely hidden in the secret compartment. It seemed so obvious to her where she had to be. But after Daniel and Sam had constructed the cabinet together, and Georgie had borrowed some fabric from Maria to make the curtains, the last rehearsal had somehow stopped everyone in the theatre dead. Sam had been sworn to secrecy, and well-paid for his trouble, and all he did was smirk as the whispers ran round the wings. No one else knew.

Lily risked a deeper breath as she felt Georgie spin

the cabinet to prove there was no secret mechanism on the other side. The cabinet was empty, even though they had all seen her climb in.

'The demon has swallowed her up! My poor little assistant...'

Lily sniffed, but cautiously. She found the patter for this bit embarrassing, she preferred the funnier parts of the act, where Daniel made handkerchiefs change colour, and Henrietta stole them, trailing a whole line of handkerchiefs after her as she raced offstage.

'Now, we must call her back from the demon's clutches...'

Lily yawned, and tried not to twitch her toes. Georgie had drawn the gauzy curtains across the empty cabinet, ready for the next part of the trick, and now the eerie music was building to the drum roll. Lily folded down the side panel, and lit the candle, hissing as the match burned her fingers. She could hear the gasps from the audience as the cabinet began to glow with a ghostly light, and she curled her fingers into demon talons, pouncing and clawing in front of the candle, casting nightmarish shadow patterns on the curtain across the front. Daniel screamed a string of meaningless words, and she blew the candle out, and the terrifying claws disappeared. The music stopped abruptly as she did it – the conductor had a mirror that meant he could see the stage, even from the orchestra pit – and for a moment there was a panicked silence in the theatre.

Then the music began again, a gentle, wheedling tune, as Daniel made mystical passes across the front of the curtain – just in case it flapped while Lily was wriggling out of her hiding place. Georgie drew back the curtain with a flourish, and Lily waved and smiled at the astounded audience as Daniel lifted her down.

The Demon's Cabinet was the finale of the act, and they bowed again and again, as the applause echoed round the theatre, before the curtains finally drew closed once more, and they raced off into the wings.

Maria hugged them delightedly, and Sam, standing by to haul up the next scenery change, clapped Lily on the back. 'You did it perfect, Lily! Hear them shouting?'

Lily turned back to the empty stage. It was true – the clapping was even louder, and now there was shouting, and stamping too.

'We haven't an encore!' Daniel murmured worriedly.

'An encore!' someone snapped. Mrs Lacey, Lydia's mother, stood by with her hands on Lydia's shoulders, while Lydia pouted prettily at Daniel. 'Nonsense. Lydia is waiting to sing. You can't disappoint her audience.'

Daniel looked as though he was about to argue, but since they hadn't rehearsed another trick, he simply bowed, and allowed Lydia, in a sparkly fairy outfit, complete with crystal-studded wings and a wand, to run on to the stage.

'We should have ended the show,' he murmured, watching as the curtains opened and the audience muttered sadly. 'But it's in her contract that she has the final song...'

Lydia was very, very good, Lily had to admit, watching as the other girl charmed the audience, making them hers again. But she wasn't quite good enough to make them forget Daniel's act. It was the magic they were sure they'd seen that they would be discussing as they left the theatre, not the Silver Songbird. And as Lydia curtseyed and ran off the stage, her flushed cheeks and gritted teeth made it quite obvious that she knew that – and she was furious.

'You're in the newspaper, Lily! Tea?' Sam was boiling a kettle over the little spirit stove in the stagehands' cubby as Lily wandered past him yawning the next morning. Their act only took about twenty minutes, but it had left her exhausted, and at the same time wound up like a clock spring. She had wriggled and tossed under their covers until Henrietta and Georgie had threatened to send her to sleep in the wardrobe room.

'Oh, please.' Lily nodded, and then she gathered what Sam had said. 'In the newspaper?'

'With a sketch, look. You in the cabinet. And Henrietta on the top of it, not that she is ever in the act. They got the dimensions wrong too,' he grumbled, but Lily could tell he was immensely proud of his creation. 'Must have given a description to the artist. Ought to tell Daniel to get that photographer we had once back to take your pictures, you could be selling them as souvenirs soon, I expect.'

Lily glanced up at him, puzzled. 'What does that mean?'

'You are an odd one, sometimes.' Sam shook his head at her, smiling. 'You and that little polished devil of a dog.' He tickled Henrietta behind the ears as he said this, and his voice was honeyed with love. Henrietta looked smugly sideways at Lily, and closed her eyes blissfully.

'I've just never heard of it – what you said,' Lily admitted humbly. 'Do you mean selling our photographs? Would people really buy them?'

'If the act carries on like this, course they will. Add a bit of cash to your running-away fund, that might.'

Lily lifted her eyes from the newspaper slowly, her heart suddenly thudding, but Sam was still smiling. Just one of his enormous furry eyebrows was raised at her.

'Course, you might not want your faces all over

town. I'm not asking, Lily, love. Sometimes you do what you need to, that's how it goes.'

'We had to,' Lily whispered. 'Really we did.'

'Like I said. I'm not asking. You be careful though. I worked for Mr Daniel's uncle, like a lot of the stage crew did, and he never mentioned no cousins to me.'

'Distant cousins...' Lily said pleadingly. 'Almost estranged.'

'Well then. You stick to that.' Sam nodded at her. 'What's it say then, in that article?'

Lily gulped, and fixed her eyes on the caption under the drawing. Her mouth curved in an absurd little smile, as she read it out loud. '*The Amazing Danieli, and the Northern Princesses, with friend, at the Queen's Theatre.* That's really us! It's a very good portrait of Henrietta, but it doesn't look like me or Georgie or Daniel at all.'

Sam laughed to himself. 'Doesn't matter. You run out and buy another couple of papers, Lily. Then you can go wafting them around, especially in front of Miss Lydia and her ma. Notice the article doesn't mention *her*. They'll be having kittens.'

'It mentions the Sandersons though. And it says the Flying Vandinis are remarkable.' Lily skimmed the rest of the article, which was mostly favourable, although it dropped heavy hints that the Queen's Men might be interested in what was going on at the Queen's. 'Will everyone be angry that it's all about us?'

Sam looked thoughtful. 'Not likely, I'd say. It's all publicity for the theatre, and everyone wants the show to do well, they'll only be out of work if it runs at a loss. No one wants the law turning up though. We might have got away with it for a bit longer without this. Still... We'll be full tonight. And the Queen's Men can't prove any of it was real magic.'

Lily looked at him sideways. She had a feeling Sam knew more than he let on.

'Because of course it wasn't,' he added. Then there was a hopeful little silence, but Lily only nodded.

'Lily! Sam! Look at this!' Daniel erupted into the tiny room, waving the newspaper and grinning so widely that Lily thought she could see every tooth in his head. 'Isn't it lucky I've thought up an encore!'

'Have you?' Lily asked wearily. 'Do I have to get squished again?'

Daniel shook his head apologetically. 'No, I'm very sorry, Lily, but I think Georgie would be better for this one. I'm going to have to pretend to enchant her, and Georgie looks more...more...'

'Dazed?' Lily suggested.

'Well, yes. I think she'd be better at looking as though she were in a trance.'

Henrietta snorted, which sounded very like a laugh. She couldn't talk in front of Sam, but she rolled her eyes at Lily.

'Do you think you could build me a lifting apparatus by tonight?' Daniel asked Sam hopefully.

'No.'

'Oh… Tomorrow?' Daniel looked hopefully at him, and Sam sighed. 'Maybe. What's it for?'

'I'm going to levitate her – lift her up in the air, like she's floating! Here, look!' He tucked the newspaper under his arm and pulled out a sheaf of drawings, unrolling them and practically filling the room.

'Well, that's not going to work, Mr Daniel, I can tell you that for sure…'

Lily slipped out of the door, and neither of them noticed she was gone. She went out into the alley behind the theatre, heading for one of the newspaper boys. Perhaps she should find a book, like an album, to stick their cuttings in? But that only made her think of Mama's photograph album, and a sudden wave of shadow and fear rose up around her so quickly that she had to stop, and lean against the wall, swallowing hard so as not to be sick.

Georgie had had no more strange trances, and Lily had managed to put Merrythought out of her mind for most of the last week. But all of a sudden it was as though she was back there again. Lily shivered, and wiped a hand over her damp forehead, pulling herself away from the wall with an effort.

She hurried on, hardly noticing where she was going, Henrietta trotting anxiously at her heels. Eventually Henrietta scurried forward a little faster, circling round in front of Lily, and snapping at her, so that she almost tripped over.

'Oh!' Lily glanced around fearfully, suddenly realising that she had no idea where they were – except that she was in the middle of a street full of smart shops. But at least the horrible sick feeling had gone. She gulped, and whispered, 'Thank you…' to Henrietta, who gave her a disapproving look, and stared round meaningfully at the people striding past.

Lily crouched down and picked her up. She was so warm and solid, and she smelled comfortingly of dog. 'Do you know where we are?' she breathed.

'Of course. We're a long way from the theatre, though. Turn down this road.' Henrietta hissed the words into Lily's hair.

Lily nodded, thinking suddenly how lucky it was that Aunt Arabel had chosen a pug for a pet, and quite a small one at that. It would have been much harder to disguise a talking wolfhound.

Suddenly Henrietta tensed, her claws digging into

Lily's shoulder. 'Something's coming,' she hissed. 'Something bad is coming. Lily, hide.'

Lily looked around the street wildly. Where on earth should she go? And what was she hiding from?

And then she saw. Gliding through the crowd of passers-by, a black, veiled figure.

Her heart thudding, Lily reached behind her to open the door of the shop they were passing, her fingers slipping and trembling. She slid inside, and clicked it shut, watching wide-eyed as Marten swept past, her veiled head turning slowly from side to side. For a moment, Lily couldn't tell what the spell-creature was doing. But then she realised, Marten was sniffing. Hunting them out, her and Georgie.

Lily pressed her hand across her mouth, suddenly certain that she really would be sick this time. Marten paused, staring around, for a horribly long time – and then she set off again, with that strange gliding walk that suggested something other than feet under her long black skirts.

Of course, she had known that Marten would have followed them to London. It was why she'd wanted to stay so close to the theatre all this time. But now she knew for certain, it was different. She felt like a helpless little rabbit, like Bella, lost and waiting for a ravenous fox.

Mama's servant-creature was quartering the city, tracking them by scent.

'It was,' Lily said stubbornly. 'You weren't there, Georgie. I know it was her.' She'd decided she had to tell her sister now. It wasn't safe to keep her in the dark, as they had back at Lacefield station.

'But how could Mama have found us so quickly?' Georgie asked, her voice doubtful. When Lily dashed back into the theatre, she had been admiring the drawing of herself in the newspaper, which one of the contortionists had given her. Now she was pleating it anxiously between her fingers.

'She hasn't!' Lily sighed crossly. 'I told you, we were miles away from the theatre. Although, I suppose she might have followed me from here... No. She went on – perhaps she caught the scent, but she couldn't work out where I was. Henrietta's sure she didn't follow us back.' She looked over Georgie's shoulder. 'Thank goodness that drawing doesn't look in the least like us. Even if Mama is here with Marten, she wouldn't recognise us from that.'

'You drew a lot of attention last night,' Henrietta muttered. They were tucked away behind some bits of scenery in the wings, where Lily had dragged them to hide. No one could see Henrietta to realise she was talking.

'So did you!' Georgie snapped. 'We all agreed to this. I was the one who said it was too dangerous, if you remember, and you two persuaded me!' She patted the painted canvas next to her, running her fingers over a foolish-looking sheep from the set for Lydia's shepherdess song. 'I don't want to run again,' she whispered. 'We can't. We haven't anywhere else to go! We were so lucky to find the theatre—'

'Luck had nothing to do with it,' Henrietta snapped.

Georgie nodded. 'I know that really. But all the same, I can't bear to start all over again. We'll just have to be watchful. It's like you said, Lily, it might be coincidence that she was so close. If we see her again, then we'll – we'll do something.'

Lily nodded. She didn't want to leave the theatre either. But she was frowning. *Something* didn't sound like a very good plan to her. Whatever they had to do, she was almost sure that Georgie would need to use her magic again, and that meant anything might happen.

Lily smiled to herself grimly. At least they could make sure it happened to Marten.

'Whatever are you lot doing hiding behind here?' Daniel peered around the scenery, staring at them.

Lily jumped. 'Don't creep up on people like that! I nearly died.'

Daniel looked horrified. 'I didn't mean to –

whatever's the matter, Lily? You've gone white. I can't have scared you that much, surely?'

'Sorry,' Lily muttered. 'I had a shock. Before...' She swallowed. 'I saw Mama's servant, Marten. In the street, not close – but she was looking for us. Mama wants us back... We knew she would, but we felt so safe here. We lost her,' she added. 'She didn't come anywhere near the theatre.'

Daniel nodded, but he was frowning. 'Just a coincidence then?' he asked.

'I really hope so. She must have been searching all over the city.' Lily shivered, thinking of Marten's horrid sniffing.

Daniel stared down at Georgie, as though he hadn't looked at her properly before. 'You two can't stay hidden here all the time, though. It's not good for you. You haven't been out since you arrived, have you?' he demanded, putting his hand under Georgie's chin, and turning her face this way and that. 'You're as pale as milk. Watered milk, even.'

'She hasn't been anywhere,' Lily agreed, and Georgie scowled at her.

'Right. Then today, I'm taking you all to watch the parade. There'll be thousands of people lining the streets, no servant of your mother's will spot you.' Daniel gave a determined nod. 'You girls deserve a treat, after the work you've been putting in.'

'What parade?' Henrietta nosed him curiously.

'Coronation Day. Every year, Queen Sophia rides in a carriage from the palace to the cathedral, for a service of thanksgiving.'

'Queen Sophia? We could *see* her?' Lily asked, only half believing him.

'Of course.'

Lily stared blankly at the canvas of the scenery in front of them. The queen. It had been on the queen's orders that their father had been taken, imprisoned, they didn't even know where. It was the queen that Georgie had been supposed to kill, with dreadful spells that she'd spent years learning. Queen Sophia was bound into their lives with magic they did not understand – but they had never seen her.

Georgie smiled wearily. 'I can wear my hat.'

Lily blinked. 'What?'

'My hat. Maria gave it to me – and some silk flowers, she showed me how to fasten them on. There's one for you too, Lily, but I haven't anything to decorate it with yet.'

'I don't mind,' Lily said impatiently. 'You'll come then?'

'It would be nice to go out. If we're sure it's safe…' Georgie nodded, looking around at the dusty sets.

There was very little light anywhere in the theatre, Lily realised suddenly. No daylight. No wonder Georgie was miserable, she told herself crossly.

'Marten doesn't know where we are. It was luck that she was close, that's all.'

'Come on then!' Daniel clapped his hands. 'Five minutes. I'll put my best waistcoat on.'

They gathered at the front of the theatre, a strange feeling of excitement making Lily and Georgie giggle, and Henrietta chase her tail, and snap at imaginary flies. They were off on a jaunt, in their nicest clothes.

'I know a good place, not too busy,' Daniel explained, hurrying them along the street. 'But we haven't got long, they'll leave the palace at ten.'

As they came towards the broader, grander streets that were on the route of the procession, crowds were gathering all around them. 'People sleep on the pavement, to get the very best places,' Daniel explained. 'Not as many as there used to be, though.' He noticed Lily's confused look. 'She's popular, Queen Sophia, but her mother isn't. Old Queen Adelaide. The Dowager.'

'She's the one who was married to King Albert? The king who was killed by Marius Grange?' Lily asked, wanting to make sure.

'That's it. And she's the one who hates magic. She always did, even before the king was assassinated.

She's the one who controls the Queen's Men, people say. She's nearly ninety, the old queen, and her wits are going. Ah, listen!'

Dimly, in the distance, they could hear the sound of cheering, and a jingling, and a thudding of hooves.

'They're coming.' Daniel grabbed their hands, and hurried them on. 'Up here, look.' He caught Lily round the waist, and boosted her and Henrietta up onto the plinth of a statue, a tall dark stone figure of a disapproving man. Lily was almost sure his frowning brows furrowed even more as she and Georgie helped to haul Daniel up after them, just in time to see a troop of horse guards trot around the bend in the road.

Cheering erupted all around the girls, so that they seemed to be floating on a cloud of sound, and a golden carriage rolled towards them. Lily clutched at the stone boot of the statue, and leaned forward, desperate to see. The carriage shone, its windows glittering like jewels in a golden setting, and she hissed crossly. Then as the carriage drew level with them, a cloud passed across the sun, and for a moment, the glare died away. Lily stared across the crowd below, into the carriage itself.

She wasn't sure how she'd expected a queen to look. Bigger, perhaps? Haughtier? More like Mama, she realised suddenly, a surprised smile twitching the corner of her mouth. Certainly not this thin-faced, worried-looking lady, waving graciously at her well-wishers. She was dressed in a rich, old-fashioned dark velvet cloak, with a fur collar, and a little tiara sat on her faded hair. None of it suited her.

'She was pretty, once...' Daniel murmured to her. 'Like a fairy princess, so they say. You wouldn't think so now, would you?'

Lily shook her head. It was confusing. Queen Sophia had broken her family, but Lily couldn't hate her. There was something familiar about her too, but Lily couldn't pin down what it was.

As the carriage rolled past, the queen leaned sideways a little, to wave at the crowd on the other side of the road, and the other occupant of the carriage was revealed.

'That's the Dowager,' Daniel muttered. 'Mad as a coot, she is.'

Lily gasped. Queen Adelaide was very old, very thin, and had a nose like the beak of an eagle. Her eyes had something of the ferocity of a bird of prey, as well. Even though she looked nothing like her, she reminded Lily strongly of her mother. It was the determination, Lily decided, huddling back against the statue's legs, the cold-blooded certainty that she was right, shining out of those dark, glinting eyes.

All of a sudden, Lily knew why she'd felt she recognised the younger queen. Sophia had such a look of Georgie – worn out from trying for years to please an impossible mother.

As the carriage went on past, and another company of glittering horsemen trotted after it, the crowd began to disperse, leaving a litter of trampled flags and coloured bunting.

Daniel jumped down, and lifted Lily and Georgie after him. They began to stroll back towards the theatre through the maze of back alleys, Lily questioning Daniel about the queen.

'She's never married then? There isn't a king?'

Daniel shook his head. 'No, her younger sister is the heir, Princess Lucasta.'

'Lily…'

A whisper behind her. Lily stopped suddenly, her legs wobbling. There was something awful in Georgie's voice, even though it was so quiet she'd hardly heard it. 'What is it?' She threw her arms round Georgie. Her sister was so pale she'd gone grey, like a stone child.

'Look.' Georgie nodded very faintly towards the other side of the road. There was a dark spot among the holiday finery of the crowd, a figure swathed in black, its head turning slowly from side to side.

'Marten,' Lily and Georgie breathed together, and

then Henrietta snapped at Lily's ankles.

'Go. Go! But don't run.'

'Who is it?' Daniel hissed.

'Move. We'll tell you later. Slowly, slowly, don't let her notice us.' Lily grabbed his hand, and hauled Georgie along with an arm around her waist. 'We have to get back to the theatre. Quickly!'

'So what was all that about?' Daniel asked, as they stumbled in through a backstage door, and hurried to his office. 'Who was that woman in the black dress?'

Lily exchanged a look with Georgie as she stuffed her sister into the balding old armchair. Should they tell him everything?

'Yes.' Henrietta nudged her ankle. 'Tell him. I promise you, he smells good. You can trust him.'

Georgie nodded, staring at her feet. 'He should know what he's hiding in his theatre. What might be coming.'

'What's going on?' Daniel crouched down next to Georgie, lowering his voice to a whisper. 'Is this to do with your mother stealing your magic? Is that why you're so frightened of her? I mean, this sounds as though it's more than just her wanting you back because she misses you.'

Lily laughed, and then put her hand over her mouth. 'Sorry. We think she's plotting against the queen. Georgie has been…'

'Enchanted,' Georgie muttered.

'But we don't know why. She's been angry with Georgie for so long, because the spells weren't working properly. We think Mama was going to kill her, and start trying to use me instead.'

'What for?' Daniel asked, looking appalled.

'We think they want to make us into a magical weapon,' Lily explained. Then she added in a whisper, 'So they can assassinate the queen.'

Daniel swallowed slowly. 'Ah. With one of those flame things Georgie threw at me, the day we met?'

Everyone stared at Georgie, who shook her head miserably. 'I still don't know what it was that I did!' Then she sighed. 'But I didn't mean to, whatever it was. It took me over. I thought we'd escaped, Lily, but she's still got me, hasn't she? Since we've been away from Merrythought, I've felt free again. But that was stupid. She's controlling me, somehow.' She leaned back against the wall, her skin still greyish and her eyes stone-like. 'I'll never get away.'

'We'll take the spell off.' Lily's voice was firm, but she couldn't meet her sister's eyes. She couldn't trust her face to look as though she believed what she was saying. Georgie wasn't in control of her own magic, and Lily hardly knew any. How could they possibly defeat such an expert magician as their own mother? 'Perhaps when we find Father, he can do it…'

Georgie shook her head again. 'No. I have to hide better.' She stared at her hands, as though she hated them. 'If only I could get rid of my magic,' she whispered. 'Then Mama wouldn't want me any more.' She looked up, a spark of hope in her eyes. 'If we both did, Lily, then we'd be useless. They'd never find us, Mama and Marten. I'm sure it's the magic Marten's hunting for.'

'Are you safe here?' Daniel asked anxiously. 'Couldn't you do one of those glamour spells, like the first time I saw you?'

Georgie's stony eyes softened with tears. 'You don't understand. It's our magic she's tracking. Our mother's servant, Marten. That woman in black. I think she can sniff out magic, especially mine, because it's all been shaped – twisted – by Mama! She knows what it smells like!' She scratched at her hands hatefully. 'I wish I could tear it out of me. Lily, you have to help me. And we should take yours too, then even if they find us Mama won't want us back!'

Lily glared at her. 'We can't get rid of it, Georgie, we don't know how! And even if we could I wouldn't want to – I've only just got it, and I love it! It's mine, it's part of me!'

'I used to feel like that...' Tears spilled out of Georgie's eyes, and Lily threw her arms around her sister.

'When we break the spell you will again. For now, just don't use your magic, it's safer that way.'

'We'll hide you somehow,' Daniel muttered, looking worriedly around the room, as though he expected Marten to materialise from behind the curtains. 'I won't let anyone steal you away.'

Lily watched critically as Georgie rose up into the air. The new dress that Daniel had sweet-talked Maria into running up at the last minute fell floatily from a high waistband, and it trailed down on either side of her body, wafting dramatically, the little embroidered silver stars glittering.

Daniel was conjuring her higher and higher, beckoning her on, with sweeps of his long fingers.

'That's as far as she goes, Mr Daniel!' a loud voice yelled from behind the curtains.

Daniel's mystical gestures stopped abruptly. 'That's fine. I wouldn't be able to reach her if she were much higher anyway. Lily, remind me to talk to Signor Lucius about the music, there's a bit of squeaking from the mechanism, he's going to need flutes playing during this part, just in case.'

'Can I get down yet?' Georgie asked plaintively. 'This board is really hard.' They had been rehearsing the new trick since Sam had finished building the mechanism, the day after the Coronation parade, and their sighting of Marten. Lily and Georgie had thrown themselves into the work, glad to think about something else, but after two solid days of pretending to be in a trance, Georgie was becoming mutinous.

'How are you going to prove that there isn't something behind the curtain lifting her?' Lily demanded. 'I don't think it's going to be hard for people to work it out.'

'Aha!' Daniel darted into the wings and came back with a child's hoop, the kind that Lily had seen little boys bowling through the park when she had gone exploring. 'Watch! Oh, and tonight, Lily, when I snap my fingers, can you bring this out to me? Now look… Remember the audience don't know that we've let down the extra curtain this far forward, they'll think this is the back of the stage. See the hoop?' He held it up in one hand, passing it slowly, surely, all round Georgie, wafting it suspensefully around her, and staring out into the imaginary audience with dark, brooding eyes.

Lily came closer. 'Do it again,' she asked, puzzled, and Daniel laughed, and passed the hoop around Georgie's wafting skirts once more.

'Hurry up!' Georgie moaned. 'I've got the most dreadful crick in my neck.'

'Did you see?'

'Has it got a hole in it, so the bar can get through?' Lily asked, staring suspiciously at the hoop.

'No! But if you think that, perhaps I should pass it into the audience first, so they can test it, that might add a little something.' He scribbled a note to himself. 'Watch again.'

'Oh!' Lily laughed, genuinely impressed. 'I saw it that time, Daniel, that's really clever. I would have sworn blind that you passed it all round her!'

Daniel made her a little bow. 'Yes, yes, I'm sorry, Georgie. Bring her down, Sam. So. You think it'll work, as our grand finale?'

Georgie sat up, wriggling her shoulders. 'Did I really look as though I was floating?'

Lily nodded. 'It was very impressive. Even better with music, and that special mist stuff, I should think. But Daniel, if this is to be the grand finale, what happens to Lydia's fairyland song?'

Daniel bit his lower lip. 'Mmm. That's my next job. Breaking it to Mrs Lacey that little Lydia's contract specifies she's allowed the final song – and she'll have it.' He grinned slyly at Lily. 'Well, I don't sing. Do you?'

'She'll spifflicate you…' Lily whispered. It was one of

Sam's young apprentice Ned's favourite words, and although Lily wasn't sure exactly what it meant, she liked it.

Daniel shrugged. 'After the reaction from the audience the last three nights, and the reviews we've had, she hasn't a leg to stand on.'

Lily nodded. He was right, but Lydia and her mother would never admit it. She decided that after the performance tonight, she would ask Georgie how to cast a protection spell. Maria had told them some dreadful stories about jealousy in the theatre, after she'd found Georgie in tears when Lydia had caught her alone, and mercilessly demolished the dancing she did in their act. Lily had no intention of letting Lydia get away with any of those sort of tricks. Jamming a pin down inside one of Georgie's greasepaint sticks was just the sort of thing she could imagine Lydia trying. And the little toad would be gushingly sympathetic when Georgie tore a scratch across her cheek.

'Come on. We need to clear the stage. We sent everyone away so we could rehearse this, remember, and they're all fretting. People want a last run-through before tonight.' A wide, fake smile spread across Daniel's face as a large figure barrelled its way down the aisle like a rhinoceros. In a corset. 'Mrs Lacey! I was just coming to find you…'

*

Lily ran gracefully – or as gracefully as she could – back onto the stage with the hoop, which had been painted silver now to make it look more mystical, and handed it to Daniel. Daniel twirled it in his hands, and stepped towards the edge of the stage, swirling it through the air to demonstrate to the audience how solid it was. Then he walked back to Georgie, apparently floating in a deep trance above the stage, and started the clever sleight of hand that made the hoop appear to pass around her body. Lily smiled a little. Now she knew how he did it, it was easy to see – but the audience were sighing with amazement. They were convinced Daniel had levitated the Northern Princess, and excited whispers were running around the theatre. This was even better than the other girl disappearing in the cabinet.

His face still deathly serious – though Lily could tell he was longing to grin – Daniel began to beckon Georgie down, while Lily kneeled at the foot of the platform, trying to look enthralled. She was close enough to the mechanism to hear a sudden squeak, and a crack. Daniel heard it too – she could see his hands jolt as he tried to work out what was going on, and he glanced behind him with his eyebrows practically in his hair. Georgie's foot twitched anxiously, and she slid forwards a little. She was sliding off the board, Lily realised in horror, although to the audience it only looked as if Daniel's spell was slipping. He redoubled his mystical gestures, and hissed to Sam behind the curtain. 'Hurry! Get her down!'

'The joist's cracking! Someone's sawn it half-through!' Sam hissed back. 'I bring her down any faster and it'll split!'

Georgie was keeping almost perfectly still, her hands crossed over her chest, but Lily could see her eyelids fluttering, and knew that she was panicking. Should she fall, and ruin the act she'd worked so hard for, or use just a little of her magic to save herself? Georgie adored the act, playing up to her Northern Princess image of frosty grace. It would be terrible to fall in front of a packed house. And it would expose the trick.

Lily swallowed. What if something dreadful happened? What if Georgie exploded the entire audience this time, not just a chair? And how much magic was it safe to use before Marten scented them again?

A faint silvery shimmer was rippling the long gauzy skirts now, as Georgie started a spell to hold herself up – and Lily caught Henrietta's horrified expression, and knew they couldn't risk it.

She stood up, forcing herself to do it slowly, and ran to Daniel's side, mimicking his gestures as if she was desperately adding extra power to his spell – as though this was such difficult magic that he needed her help.

'Georgie, let me!' she breathed, and for a second the silvery shimmer faded, and then grew stronger, as Lily sealed the splintering wood of the joist with a binding spell that probably meant no one would ever be able to cut through it again. Every fibre of the wood remembered the tree it had grown in, and bound itself together like hardened oak.

The audience sighed blissfully as a cloud of silver dust joined the chemical smoke that Ned had been pumping out from behind the curtain, and Georgie came back down to the platform, and allowed herself to be woken from her trance with only the slightest hint of a glare at Daniel.

Then they ran to the edge of the stage, and bowed, and bowed again, as the audience thundered their applause. But Lily was too angry to appreciate the storm of clapping and the cheers. She simply wanted to get off the stage, so she could go and wring a little songbird's neck.

TWELVE

Lydia was standing in the wings, her face grey under the greasepaint. Lily had been planning to – to – she wasn't quite sure what, but she could guarantee Lydia wouldn't have liked it.

But the other girl's shocked face stopped her, and she lunged for Henrietta's collar, as the little pug was growling furiously. Of course. Lydia had never really believed their act was magical. But now she'd seen Lily rescue Georgie, and she knew that Lily had used magic – because she had been the one who sabotaged the lift.

Georgie grabbed Lily's arm, and pulled her back. 'What are we going to say?' she hissed.

Lily hugged her, half out of relief that she hadn't been hurt, and half to hide what she was about to say. 'I think she knows. But we can't admit it. We just have to pretend it was an accident, and we were lucky to get away with it.' She glanced up at Daniel, who was coming offstage behind them, and he nodded, although he looked angry.

He quickly smoothed his frown into a worried look, and caught Georgie's shoulders. 'Georgie! Are you all right? I don't understand what happened, there must have been a fault in the mechanism. I'm so sorry!'

Georgie shook her head, and leaned against him. She looked frightened, and not at all magical. Lily could see that it was because Georgie didn't know what to say, but it worked. All the female artistes were cooing and fussing around her, and she was led off by Maria and Mrs Hopkins the Elephant Woman for a reviving cup of tea.

Sam barrelled out from behind the curtain, closely followed by Ned, his apprentice, who was looking scared. Lily eyed him, thoughtfully, and Ned turned slightly green. 'Somebody sawed through—'

Daniel drew a finger swiftly across his throat. So swiftly that Lily only saw it because she was looking.

Sam blinked, and glared at Daniel. 'I shall be having words with the timber merchant,' he muttered. 'Unreliable – hmm. Ladies present.'

'Quite.' Daniel nodded. 'We were lucky. We shall have to make sure it doesn't happen again.' He was usually such a mild-mannered and pleasant person that the icy tone of his voice came as a shock, and Lily drew closer to Sam, whose huge, bearlike bulk was suddenly comforting. Sam looked down at her doubtfully for a minute, and then he hugged her tightly against his velveteen waistcoat.

He knew, Lily realised, with a sudden jump in her stomach. He knew she'd used real magic to rescue Georgie. But he didn't care. He liked her anyway. Lily closed her eyes. She was so tired that it felt as though her bones were melting. She could hardly hold herself up. But she forced her eyes open. What were they going to do about Lydia? She knew too, now. And probably so did her mother. Lily glanced around the wings. Almost everyone had gone – only the stage crew were tidying away, resetting the scenery for the next performance. Sam's apprentice Ned was skulking in a corner, fiddling with some ropes, still looking pale and miserable.

'He's sweet on her,' Sam muttered. 'Gulpy little fool. She probably offered him a kiss.'

'You mean Ned sawed through the joist?' Lily asked, shocked. She liked Ned. He was funny, and he fed Henrietta the crusts of his sandwiches.

Daniel took a step towards Ned, his teeth showing in a wolfish sort of way.

'No!' Sam scowled, and caught his coat. 'Of course

not. If I'd thought that I'd have thrown him halfway across the street. He let her see the mechanism, though, I'll bet. *Oh, Ned, it's so clever, won't you show me how they do it?* This last was in a high, silly voice that sounded amazingly like Lydia, coming from someone as big as Sam. 'He helped me build it, you see,' Sam added gloomily. 'The master wanted it double-quick time.'

Henrietta let out a little breath of a growl, staring at the unhappy-looking boy, who was carefully not looking at them.

'Don't throw him out,' Lily begged. 'It's Lydia's fault, not his. Did you see where she went, Daniel? I don't know what she's going to do. She can't tell anyone about the spell. She only knows because she was the one who spoiled the trick. She's never going to own up to that, is she?'

Daniel shook his head. 'I don't know. Perhaps not here, in the theatre. But if she put it that she was suspicious before, and she sabotaged us as a trap…'

'Oh.' Lily nodded. 'Yes, I suppose. Then she's going to tell, isn't she?' Her heart was racing, and she glanced from side to side, like an animal in a trap. The magic inside her was straining and fluttering too. She could use it to escape, she knew she could. But then it wouldn't be only their mother who was chasing her – it would be a manhunt.

The ushers had already barred the front doors, but now there was a hammering and a shouting at the front of the theatre, and Daniel grimaced. 'That was quick. I wonder where she ran to?'

'Is that them?' Lily asked, her voice a thready squeak.

'Don't you worry, my lovely,' Sam muttered, thrusting her behind him. 'No one's going to listen to that little viper.' He couldn't quite hide the worry in his words, though, however hard he tried. He hauled on the ropes that opened the curtains, and revealed three men, two of them in black uniforms, and one in a smart overcoat, walking down the aisle, with one of the ushers hurrying after them, looking apologetically at Daniel.

'Is there something wrong?' Daniel asked, advancing to the front of the stage. 'Alfred, have we been burgled?' he asked the usher, anxiously.

'No, sir. They say they want to talk to you, and Miss Georgie and Miss Lily. About the act...'

'Really?' Daniel cast a puzzled glance at the policemen, and Lily noted it admiringly. Daniel had been an actor before he inherited his uncle's theatre, and she could see that he must have been good. He called back into the wings. 'Ned, go and fetch Miss Georgie, please.'

Ned, now looking even more miserable, nodded, and went off in the direction of the dressing rooms. The two policemen stood uncertainly in the middle of the stage, eyeing the scenery, while the stagehands worked round them with irritable grunts. The smartly dressed man strolled around the stage, examining Georgie's platform and the Demon Cabinet with particular interest.

'Would you like me to show you anything?' Daniel asked helpfully, but the man shook his head. 'I'll wait for all the young ladies to be present.' His voice was light, and sweet, and he sounded rather aristocratic. He glanced back down into the auditorium, and Lily saw with a surge of fury that Lydia and her mother were coming in. Lydia had taken off her make-up, and was wearing one of her more sober dresses, a sailor outfit that made her look her actual age. She had clearly decided she'd look more innocent that way.

Georgie came back onto the stage. Obviously Ned hadn't kept his message quiet, as half the acts were following her, crowding curiously into the wings, and staring at the police, and the officer of the Queen's Men, who looked somewhat taken aback. Georgie hurried over to Lily and took her hand. 'What's the matter? Ned only said the police were here.'

'Miss Georgie Lancing?' the man in the overcoat asked. They had given it out that they were Daniel's distant cousins, and so they'd borrowed his surname.

Georgie nodded anxiously.

'And Miss Lily Lancing? Mr Daniel Lancing?'

Daniel drew himself up to his full height – which was very high, much taller than the officer, who was a small, slim man. But it didn't seem to worry him.

'I am Edward Hope. I represent Her Majesty, Queen Sophia, serving on her special commission in search of outlawed practices.'

'He's one of the Queen's Men,' someone whispered in the wings, and there was a sudden anxious hissing, as the words went round the crowd.

Edward Hope only smiled faintly, as if a small child was misbehaving, and he was pretending not to see. 'We have had…a report. About your theatre, Mr Lancing. About your act, in particular.'

Daniel nodded, smiling back. 'I had wondered if your department would become interested,' he admitted, shrugging a little. 'I suppose we ought to take it as a compliment, girls, don't you think?'

Lily nodded, and tried to smile, but she wasn't nearly as good an actor as he was.

'You deny it, then? That you're using forbidden practices?'

Daniel snorted. 'Real magic?' He leaned forward, and pulled the handkerchief out of Edward Hope's waistcoat pocket. He did it so quickly that Hope hardly saw what was happening, and he watched bemused as a string of multicoloured handkerchiefs streamed out of his pocket, and Henrietta leaped to catch them, and chased off around the stage, before gathering them up, and sitting on her hindquarters to offer them prettily back to him.

'You see? Clever fingers, Mr Hope. And a trained dog. No magic.' Daniel smiled, and handed him back the original handkerchief.

Edward Hope leaned down to pat Henrietta. 'A very clever little creature, indeed. But what was reported to me was rather more dramatic, Mr Lancing. A girl rising into the air? One of these young ladies?'

Georgie nodded. 'Me,' she whispered nervously.

'My young assistant has had a shock tonight,' Daniel put in, very smoothly. 'Our apparatus went strangely wrong, and I'm afraid she was almost injured. It was a new trick, the first time we'd performed it. The very culmination of our art! It was extremely annoying.' He sighed. 'We are afraid the machinery was sabotaged. Someone attempted to cut through a vital piece.'

There was an angry mutter amongst those watching, and several people stepped out of the wings to glare at Lydia.

Daniel stared at her too. 'I'm only sorry, Mr Hope, if your time has been wasted out of petty spite, from a jealous performer.'

Mr Hope nodded. 'So you maintain that no magic is involved in any of your – tricks, you call them?'

'That's what they are, Mr Hope. We trick the eye. We make the audience see something that isn't there.' Daniel laughed. 'Or, more often, we hide something that is. As in the trick that went so wrong tonight. Georgie, dear one, do you think you can bear to demonstrate for Mr Hope?'

'It's mended?' Georgie asked, looking at him hesitantly. Lily could see how frightened she was. Georgie's eyes were purple, she realised, suddenly feeling far more worried about her sister than she was about any officer of the queen. If Georgie was too frightened, would she be able to control her magic?

'I promise.' Daniel blinked suddenly, realising that there was no sign of any damage on the wooden joist. 'In fact, I had Sam replace the damaged piece straight away – I was going to ask you to rehearse the trick again once you'd recovered. I know it seems cruel, Mr Hope, but we must all suffer for our art.

'Watching from the stage itself, Mr Hope, you may be able to see more clearly how the trick is managed, but I promise you, from the audience, it is most convincing.' Daniel bowed, and took Georgie by the hand, leading her to the platform, and waving his hand in front of her face, so that she seemed to fall into a deep trance, moving strangely, like some sort of clockwork doll. She lay down on the platform, her shimmering skirts trailing down the sides, and Daniel began to beckon her upwards. There was a slight but definitely audible squeak, and he grimaced apologetically at the queen's officer. 'The music covers a multitude of sins, Mr Hope. Lily, the hoop, dear, don't forget yourself.'

Lily had been watching Georgie, and hardly heard him. Surely she didn't usually let her arms swing loose like that? She looked almost dead...

Henrietta ran back onto the stage, dragging the hoop, and Mr Hope gave a little snort of laughter. He liked dogs, Lily realised thankfully. It was a point in their favour. But Georgie didn't even seem to be breathing.

'My young assistant does a most remarkable impression of a hypnotic trance, don't you think?' Daniel asked, casting a worried glance at Lily. 'And now I pass the hoop around her – like so – to make it perfectly clear that she is suspended in midair – absolutely no connection with the ground at all. Ah, did you see, Mr Hope? The clever twist of the hoop, avoiding the wooden joist?'

'It's simply a lifting mechanism?' Mr Hope came closer. 'And her dress hides the board she's lying on. Very clever, Mr Lancing. Most convincing.'

'When you bear in mind the music, and the chemical

smoke,' Daniel added apologetically. 'I'm afraid your time has been quite wasted…'

But Edward Hope was staring at Georgie, his eyebrows drawing together. He caught one of her hands, and lifted it, watching how it swung back bonelessly. 'Wake up, miss,' he told her sharply.

Georgie didn't.

She couldn't, Lily realised, running to catch her up tightly and hold her, and seeing Georgie's head roll back. Terrified by the sabotage of the trick earlier on, and arrival of the police, Georgie had disappeared inside herself, where she felt safest. Her twisted magic had sealed her away, and taken her over. Who knew what else it was planning?

'She's fainted,' Lily told Daniel. 'She's frightened, you know how highly strung she is!' She stared into his puzzled eyes, willing him to understand.

'Oh dear. Maria! Come and help us, please.' The little wardrobe mistress hurried clucking onto the stage. 'Miss Georgie's fainted again.' He shrugged apologetically at Hope. 'She's very prone to it, I'm afraid. Dramatic temperament, you know, and she was very shocked by the accident earlier on. Sam!'

Sam's bearded face poked through between the curtains, giving Hope a very good view of the lifting mechanism.

Daniel flinched. 'I do hope we can trust you, sir, not to reveal our secrets to any other theatres. Sam, could you carry Miss Georgie back to her dressing room? She's collapsed again.'

'Tch. Poor little thing,' Sam muttered, catching Georgie up, and Edward Hope watched, frowning a little, as he began to carry her away.

'No!' The shout came from below the stage, where Lydia was standing in front of the first row of chairs. 'Don't you see? They're hiding it from you! She cast a spell, Lily did it. The younger one, I told you! She must have done, I cut it almost through…' She trailed off, as Sam advanced to the edge of the stage, looking more bearlike than ever.

'It was you, then, was it! Trying to break my machinery? You could have half killed her!'

'Little vixen,' Maria called angrily. 'Jealous spite, that's what it is, because Miss Georgie got her picture in the paper.'

'Don't you speak about my Lydia like that! My golden-voiced angel, jealous of some nasty trickster!' Mrs Lacey's chins wobbled as she screamed back, and various other performers surged forward to tell her just what they thought of her.

Daniel shook his head sorrowfully. 'All so highly strung,' he explained to Mr Hope.

'Hmm.' Mr Hope stepped back delicately, as though he thought someone might soil his shoes. 'It does seem to have been an unfortunate – misunderstanding. But do be careful, Mr Lancing, won't you? Your act does run a rather fine line.'

Daniel nodded, and Lily held her breath as Mr Hope strolled down the front steps, followed by the policemen, and made his way out of the theatre. Then she turned back to Georgie, patting her hands the way she'd tried before. But someone else pulled her away.

'She is under a spell! I tell you she *is*! Why can't any of you see?' Lydia seized Georgie's face between her hands, and then slapped her cheek hard.

'Don't you dare!' Lily yelled, reaching for her, but Sam got there first, back-handing Lydia out of the way, as if she were a fly. He did it very gently – she would have been on the other side of the stage if he'd been really trying – but even so she fell over, landing clumsily in a heap of petticoats.

'Oh!' she screamed, and weeping in angry frustration, she pushed her way angrily across the stage, blundering towards the wings.

'Be careful! Miss Lydia!' Ned started after her, but he was too late. She was already pulling at the rope she'd somehow wrapped around her ankle, pulling at it furiously, wanting to get away from the eyes and the whispers, and the angry accusations.

The metal bar seemed to fall terribly slowly, Lily thought, watching it twirl gently, almost gracefully down to the stage, where Lydia stood gaping upwards.

Daniel started to run forward, and so did half-a-dozen others, but none of them could possibly reach her in time. Sam swung round, reaching out one helpless arm, trailing Georgie from the other.

And then the bar wasn't there any more, and a shower of tiny glowing sparks fell to the stage, dying out to a fine black dust that settled on everyone's clothes.

Lily smiled from pure relief, the agonising strain of the magic inside her gone for the moment. Georgie, leaning against Sam's shoulder, beamed back dazedly, woken out of her trance as Lily seized her magic too, and hurled it at the bar.

She had no idea what they'd done, again, Lily realised, her smile dying away. And this time, there was no hiding it. The whole theatre had seen them save Lydia, and Edward Hope could be only half a street away – perhaps a little more, if they'd had a carriage outside the door. Still, it wouldn't take five minutes to call him back.

She turned, measuring the distance to the door, and felt Henrietta pressing against her leg, shivering. Could they run? Was there any point? Exploding the rigging bar had taken all the magic she could find. She hadn't had a proper thought of a spell, she'd simply flung her magic and hoped, and taken Georgie's with her. She had nothing left, not for a while.

She glanced apologetically at Daniel, who stared back at her, white-faced and horrified.

Alfred Sanderson, the red-headed trick cyclist, was the first to step forward, and Lily flinched. He was the one who had admired Henrietta's timing. It seemed worse somehow, that such a nice man should be the one to condemn them.

But Alfred looked around the silent crowd, and shook his head, as he hauled Lydia up. 'You want to be a sight more careful, missy. You could have hurt yourself, running all over the stage. What if there'd been something on the end of that rope, hmm? Could have done yourself a damage.'

His brothers nodded. 'Not that it wouldn't have served her right,' the youngest one added. 'Nasty spiteful little cat. I hope you're not planning on keeping her on the bill, Mr Daniel?'

Daniel shook his head, his mouth half-open. Then he seemed suddenly to wake up, and he turned to glare at Lydia's mother, who was standing at the edge of the stage, white-faced and shaking. 'I'm terminating your contract. I'll pay you till the end of the month.'

She shook her head as if to protest, and he advanced on her, snarling. 'Be glad I don't sue you for malicious slander! Get out of my theatre, and take that little brat with you!'

A path opened up across the stage, as everyone drew themselves away from Lydia and her mother, and they scurried away, stooping and ashamed, and everyone else followed after them, patting Henrietta as they went, or pinching Lily's cheek affectionately, till the girls were left alone on the stage with Daniel.

Lily hugged her sister tightly. 'I was so afraid,' she whispered. 'I didn't know what you might do, when you started that spell in the middle of the act.'

Georgie shook her head. 'Neither did I.' She swallowed sadly. 'Lily, I don't know if we can stay here. It's too dangerous. We have to go, and try to find Father, so we can get rid of whatever Mama's put inside me. What if I – I might hurt someone... But where can we go?'

'I don't know. I'd only just started to feel that we belonged here,' Lily said miserably.

Daniel sighed. 'Don't tell me I've just got rid of the Silver Songbird, and now you two are walking out.'

'We'll help you train up a couple of the ballet dancers,' Lily promised him. 'They'll do it now they know the act's a success. Probably better than we did.

And we'll help you think up some more tricks first. You do see that Georgie's right, don't you? We have to go. We can't risk the Queen's Men coming back. You can't risk it either. That Hope man was still suspicious.'

'Shall we go abroad?' Henrietta asked, sniffing a circle around the three of them excitedly. 'I've always fancied the continent.'

'Magic isn't outlawed abroad,' Daniel agreed thoughtfully. 'You might be better off out of the country, for all I hate the thought of losing you. But how are we going to get you there? You can't go off travelling on your own, not overseas.'

'Lily!' Georgie gasped suddenly. 'We've forgotten Marten!'

Lily stared at her for a few seconds, still so caught up in the performance and Lydia's dramatic rescue that she hardly knew what Georgie was saying.

Georgie leaned forward and shook her. 'All that magic we used to save Lydia! She'll be able to tell where we are, I'm sure she will. We have to get away. Now!'

Lily nodded, suddenly out of ideas. 'Where can we go? Could we hide at the museum again?' She faltered.

'Let's just get away from here,' Henrietta raced across the stage, and then back again to tug at Lily's skirts. 'Come on!'

'I'll come with you. We can go to my sister's house,' Daniel suggested. 'It's far enough away from the theatre. Or do you leave a trail?' he asked helplessly. 'I don't know about these things...'

'Neither do we,' Lily gave a little half-laugh.

They hurried out into the alleys behind the theatre, and Daniel raced ahead. 'I'll find a cab.'

Lily was nodding gratefully, about to turn back to her sister to say how lucky they were to have him to help them.

But then there was a strangled little noise behind her, and Henrietta whirled around, barking madly.

Lily turned to see Georgie struggling against the black-gloved hand across her mouth, trying to wrench herself from the grip of the black arms.

'Marten!' Lily threw herself at her sister, but the spell-creature hissed, and Lily dropped back in horror, seeing that she had claws, piercing the black gloves, and scratching at Georgie's throat.

'Georgie, fight her!' Lily whispered. 'Stop her, a spell, now, you must!'

But Georgie shook her head. Her blue eyes were round with terror over the black glove.

Daniel had come pelting back, white-faced. 'Why won't she do anything?' he asked angrily, his fists clenched. 'Can't she use magic on her – that thing...'

Lily could see he was longing to fight, but had no idea how to deal with such a creature.

'She can't...' Lily told him miserably, as she realised it herself. 'I used all her magic, to save Lydia. She hasn't any left. I haven't either.' She stretched out her arms to Georgie, and there was no glad rush of power into her fingers.

Daniel lunged forward, but Lily seized his arm, hauling him back. 'No! Look at the claws! We can't fight for her, Marten will slice her to ribbons. Mama won't care what she looks like. Georgie, find something inside! You have to,' she screamed at her sister frantically.

'I've only got Mama's awful spells left,' Georgie whimpered. 'I can't use them. I don't know what they'll do.'

'She'll take you *back* to Mama, Georgie. Mama will be using you again. Whatever you do can't be worse. Now!'

Georgie's eyes closed, and Lily let out a strangled howl of anger. She couldn't give up.

But she wasn't, Lily realised then. She had only been gathering her strength. A hazy silverish cloud was forming around her and Marten, a cloud of dust from the dry road. Greyish London dust, slowly forming itself into some sort of creature. Lily dug her nails into her palms. Too slowly. 'Hurry, Georgie...' she whispered.

Marten was twitching from side to side behind her veil. What instructions had she been given? Was she not allowed to kill the girl? It seemed not. Instead of digging those foul claws in deeper, she started to pull Georgie with her back down the alley, making for an eerie puddle of darkness in the shadow of an old iron staircase.

'She's taking her to Mama,' Lily whispered, creeping after them. 'Georgie, quickly!'

The greyish form grew softly pink, and Lily retched suddenly, realising that Georgie's spell was stealing her own blood to make itself stronger.

'What is that thing?' Daniel muttered.

'A monster,' Henrietta snarled.

But the monster was working. It was a wolf, Lily saw now. A huge, greyish-pink wolf, with Georgie's blood dripping from its jaws, and it was snapping eagerly at Marten, pulling at her veil, so that Lily caught a sickening glimpse of greenish spell-flesh underneath, horribly torn, and leaking foul enchantments.

'Yes!' Lily hissed, as the wolf hurled itself against Marten again, worrying at the black wrappings that were suddenly all that was left. Marten had been torn away to nothing.

'Has she really gone?' Daniel asked, staring at the limp pile of cloth.

Henrietta nodded. 'Yes. But that hasn't.'

Georgie had fallen when Marten let go of her, and now she was a crumpled little heap on the cobbles, her pretty flowered hat crushed beside her.

The dust-wolf was standing over her. It was redder still, and it was sniffing at her throat.

'Her spell's going to eat her!' Daniel yelled.

'She didn't want to...' Lily muttered. 'I made her, I shouldn't have.'

But the wolf was looking up at them now, growling angrily. Its prey had disappeared, and now there were others, circling its next meal. It lunged forward, snapping at Henrietta, who skittered back to hide shivering in Lily's skirts.

'What do we do with it?' she whined.

Lily shook her head. 'I don't know. We have to do something, and we can't just chase it away. If it runs off – it could eat a child in one gulp.'

Daniel moved forward cautiously, and Lily grabbed his arm. 'What are you doing?' she hissed.

'Shh, I've got a plan.' He shook her off. 'Stay back.'

The wolf growled lower, deep in its throat. It was fading a little, Lily realised, as the wind blew down the alleyway. It needed Georgie's blood to keep it together. Or someone's blood. It probably didn't care.

'Get it away from her!' she whispered. 'I think it'll fall apart if it doesn't...you know...feed...'

'Right.' Daniel waved his arms in front of the wolf, which watched him with hungry reddish eyes. He flicked a red handkerchief out of the hidden place in his shirt cuff, and wafted it about.

The wolf gazed hungrily at the blood-red fabric, and snarled, taking a step away from Georgie. It gathered itself on its dusty haunches, ready to spring, and Daniel threw himself back against the wall, the handkerchief fluttering down onto the stones. The wolf turned in midair to snap at it, and landed awkwardly, worrying at the scrap of red with insubstantial teeth.

Lily huddled next to Georgie, holding her tightly, and looked up at the huge grey creature as it paced back towards them, spitting scarlet threads.

'It's going,' Lily whispered. Henrietta stood in front of them, barking defiantly. 'Not fast enough,' she snapped. 'And if eats me, it'll be stronger again – strong enough to eat you too. Do something!'

Lily glanced about desperately. Daniel was pressed against the wall, scrabbling for a rock, a stick, anything to use as a weapon.

Lily had nothing. Only her magic, which she hardly knew how to use. *What settles dust?* she thought frantically.

'Weather magic!' Henrietta barked sharply. 'Like

Arabel. You can do it, Lily, you're a Powers, all of them could call the weather!'

Lily looked up at the sky, at the clear, bright blueness, and all of a sudden, the growling of the dust-wolf took on a deeper, angrier note.

'That's it!' Henrietta howled, and Lily gasped.

It was thunder growling, and the raindrops were already falling, fat hot heavy ones, splashing on the cobbles. Splashing, and stabbing little holes in the thick dust, darkening it.

The wolf twisted with fury, and its growls joined in the crash of thunder, as the rain ate away its dust-grey coat.

Then Daniel stood up, staggering, and he and Lily stared at the reddish stream running between the cobblestones, running away to nothing.

Behind them, Georgie stirred, putting her hand to her neck and wincing. 'Did it work?' she murmured vaguely. 'Did I get rid of her?'

Lily pulled her upright, and stood with her arm around her sister's waist. 'Yes. But Georgie, next time...' She tailed off, and sighed.

Georgie shivered. 'Was it bad? I almost remember – a *wolf*? I shouldn't have tried, Lily, I knew it!'

'It wasn't as bad as whatever Mama would have made you do, if Marten had dragged you back to her.' Lily shrugged. 'Georgie, don't you remember? It tore Marten to bits!' She wrapped her arms more tightly round her sister, leaning her head against Georgie's shoulder. 'You got rid of her. You actually did it. I can't believe she's gone.'

'Your mother will be furious.' Henrietta licked her chops smugly. 'A good day's work, I think.'

Georgie scowled at her. 'You're an inhuman creature, do you know that?'

Henrietta only sniffed.

'But we still have to leave,' Lily said suddenly, a little of the triumph leaking away. 'Even though Marten's gone.'

'No one at the theatre would give you away,' Daniel said pleadingly. 'Why don't you just stay? If that was your mother's best shot.'

'No. We have to find our father.' Lily traced the evil-looking scratches on her sister's neck with a delicate finger. 'He'll be able to help Georgie, I'm sure he will. We have to break that spell. It'll still be with us, otherwise. Wherever we are.'

Georgie sat up a little, stretching out her fingers, and stared at them, almost hatefully. 'I know. I can feel it inside me now. Waiting.'

'What for?' Henrietta looked up at her, the glint gone from her round black eyes.

'I simply don't know.' Georgie clenched her fingers tightly.

'We'll break it,' Lily told her, seizing Georgie's stone-like fists. 'We'll find him, and he'll know how. Then you'll be free, and you can do whatever you want with your magic. Nothing, if you like! You can come back and help Maria in the wardrobe instead, and forget all about it. Couldn't she?' she asked Daniel fiercely, and he nodded, smiling, even though he still looked sad.

'What will you do?' Georgie whispered, squeezing Lily's hand gratefully. 'When we're free?'

Lily looked at Henrietta, silenced for once. She had no idea.

Henrietta sniffed. 'Break the spell first. Then we'll decide.'

Lily nodded. 'Exactly.' She took a deep breath, and brushed the last of the pinkish mud from the skirts of her costume. She knew she had to free her sister.

Nothing else mattered.

Win!

For a chance to win one of twenty signed copies
of *Rose* by Holly Webb,
just answer the following question:

What is the name of Lily's magical dog?

Send your answer, along with
your name, address and
telephone number to:

Lily Competition
Orchard Books
338 Euston Road
London
NW1 3BH

Or email:
ad@hachettechildrens.co.uk

Competition will close
31st December 2011.
Only available to UK and Eire residents.
For full terms and conditions go to
www.orchardbooks.co.uk/TermsAndConditions.aspx

www.orchardbooks.co.uk

Questions and Answers with Holly Webb

Where did the idea for *Lily* come from?

Lily started as a sequel to my *Rose* books. I loved the world that had grown through the four books, and I didn't want to leave it. But I wanted to change it – so that magic wasn't special and amazing any more, but something that people were ashamed of instead.

Did you set out to write a historical novel?

Yes. I loved historical novels as a child and still do. My favourites were *A Traveller in Time* by Alison Uttley, and *A Little Princess* by Frances Hodgson Burnett. Rose and Lily – who both have very hard childhoods, even though they're so different – owe a lot to Sara, the main character from *A Little Princess*. I loved her story.

Characters from your earlier series *Rose* appear in *Lily* – did you intend to do this from the start?

Yes – a main character from the *Rose* books (I won't tell you the name because it might spoil it!) will appear in the second *Lily* book, and Rose herself will be in the third – but she will be fifty years older! I didn't want any of the *Rose* characters to take over the *Lily* books, but I really like the idea of the passing of time within that world.

Which idea came first: the animals or the magic?

The magic. The editor I originally discussed the *Rose* books with, when I was planning the first book, asked for 'no talking cats please.' But Gus was unstoppable...

Don't miss

Lily

and the Shining Dragons

Coming in spring 2012!

Lily and Georgie find themselves trapped in a school where magical children are hidden away.

But magic will always find a way – and the dragons are stirring...

978 1 40831 350 3 £5.99 PB
978 1 40831 641 2 £5.99 eBook

Read on for an exclusive sneak preview of
Lily and the Shining Dragons...

'Someone's watching you two.'

Lily looked up at Sam, panting a little. He'd caught her as she hurried offstage. They'd had three curtain calls, and she'd had to race back to the front of the stage and bow again and again before they could go, and let the trick cyclist troupe come on. The illusionist act seemed to be more popular every night.

'They're supposed to watch us, Sam. *Everyone's* supposed to be watching!'

'You know what I mean, missy. Don't be smart.'

Henrietta growled, very quietly, but she was eyeing Lily, not Sam. Lily stopped smiling, and shook her head. 'I won't. What do you mean? Who's watching?'

'A lady. Tall, looks like to me. Thin. *Very* thin, but not like it's natural. She's in one of the boxes, first tier, left of the stage.' He frowned. 'She's got a look of your sister, though I can't quite say how. That light hair, maybe.'

Lily went pale. 'Mama?' she faltered. But then Henrietta nipped her ankle crossly. 'Oh, no, not if she's thin. All right, I know it was stupid, Henrietta! But there's no one else...' She stopped. Actually, of course, she didn't know that. She and Georgie had always supposed they had no relatives, because Mama had never mentioned them.

'Want me to point her out?' Sam shuffled her towards the edge of the curtain.

Lily peered around it, careful not to sway the heavy velvet. The auditorium was packed, not a little crimson chair empty.

'There, see? With a boy next to her.' Sam nudged Lily, showing her a tall, regal-looking woman in one of the nearest boxes.

She had a good view there, Lily thought, the blood seeming to flow through her heart more slowly all of a sudden. A very good view. The gold-haired woman couldn't know that Lily was on the other side of the curtain. Lily would swear that she was hidden. But the woman was staring right at her. Straight into Lily's eyes.

Lily ducked back into the wings, with Henrietta coiling anxiously around her ankles, and whimpering.

'Who is she?' Sam demanded. 'You look as though you're about to faint, Lily. What's happening? Is that your ma?'

Lily shook her head. 'I don't know who she is. But you're right, she does look like Georgie. A little. She was *looking* at me, Sam. She knows who I am.' She leaned against the wall, biting her lip. 'We have to go on stage again, at the end of the show. Our finale act. She'll be watching us again.'

'And I'll be watching her. I promise you. If I see anything that looks…nasty, I'll haul you offstage. All of you. Even if it means breaking the illusion. I won't let anyone hurt you.'

'You can't do that!' Lily sounded shocked. She and Georgie and Henrietta had only been theatre performers for a few weeks, but they had absorbed how important it was to keep the audience happy. However much one hated someone offstage, onstage one smiled and laughed and acted like the best of friends. The show must always go on.

'Watch me,' Sam muttered, leaning out to try and catch another glimpse of the skinny, gold-haired woman.

Lily smiled at him. She knew that she and Georgie would have to go onstage, and wave and smile and do everything the way they usually did it. And she knew that although Sam would do anything he could to help, if the woman in the stage-left box wanted to hurt Lily or Georgie somehow, he would be worse than useless. He would probably get himself hurt too, which was another thing for Lily to worry about.

Whoever she was, she'd used magic. Lily was sure. She'd *known* that Lily was behind the curtain peering out. Only magic could have told her that, and all magic was forbidden by the Queen's Decree. The gold-haired woman was another magician in hiding. She had to be.

So even if Lily hadn't hated the idea of spoiling the show, she had to go back onstage. She had to show the gold-haired woman that she wasn't afraid, that she knew who had come to watch them. Lily would stare back, eye to eye. That way, the woman would want to meet them, surely? Then they would have what they needed. Another magician. Someone who might know where their father was.

'Is she still there?' Lily hissed to Sam, as they waited in the wings to run on for the finale.

He nodded grimly, and Lily smiled.

'What are you two planning?' Daniel asked, looking at them suspiciously, and Georgie turned worried eyes on Lily.

'There's a magician in the left-hand box.' Lily lowered her voice and nodded towards it. 'A woman. Georgie, don't go into your dying duck act! We need a magician, don't you see? She might know where Father is. Just and try and look…tempting.'

'Tempting!' Georgie hissed. 'I'm not a supper dish, Lily!'

'Not yet.' Sam exchanged a determined look with Daniel. 'I'll be watching them, don't you worry.'

'You can't.' Daniel shook his head. 'If she's a magician, we have to let Lily and Georgie protect everyone else. Lily, why didn't you say? We could have cleared the theatre. A fire. A typhus scare. Anything!'

'I didn't tell you because I knew that's what you would say!' Lily snapped. 'Especially after Marten. I don't want to get away from her, I need to ask her things.' She shook out her glittery skirts, and assumed her stage smile, the one with lots of teeth. It did not go well with the determined scowl. 'So come on. Tempting, remember?'

And the curtains drew back...

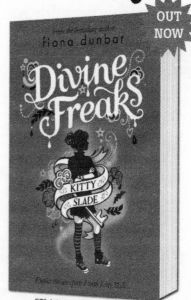